AN UNWELCOME JOURNEY

THE SOUL BOUND SAGA
BOOK ONE

JAMES E WISHER

SAND HILL PUBLISHING

Edited by: Janie Linn Dullard

Cover art by: B-Ro

ISBN: 978-1-68520-023-7

010120231.0

CHAPTER 1

Joran Den Cade held up the little alcohol burner he'd been using to heat an alembic and blew the flame out. The wick smoked and the acrid stink curled his nose. He set the burner back on his granite workbench to cool and studied the ounce of clear, odorless liquid that had collected in a glass flask under the alembic's beak. The lack of scent indicated that the first process had succeeded.

He held the flask up to the nearest alchemical light dangling from the ceiling. The golden liquid—contained in a special glass sphere nearly as hard as steel—emitted a steady glow devoid of heat. Far safer than a lantern given the flammability of some of the reagents he kept in the lab.

Three tiny black specks floated in the clear liquid. Joran ground his teeth and snarled. Another failure. He'd been so certain this time. When he prepared the flask to receive the liquid he'd taken extra care to be sure no contaminants lingered either inside or outside. No, the failure must be with the precursor. He'd filtered it three times before beginning the distillation. Maybe four would be the charm.

Considering how much money he'd spent on this experiment over the past week, it had better be.

Speaking of money, it had to be close to dinner time. During the long summer days he always lost track of how long he'd been working. Joran smiled to himself and set his most recent failure on the workbench. In truth, he frequently lost track of time year round.

He couldn't afford that today. He had to have dinner with his family tonight, a twice-monthly ritual his mother insisted on. Not that Joran minded eating at his parent's estate. Despite his father's constant nagging about adventure, seeing the world, and not wasting his youth trapped in a lab at the imperial college, Joran generally got along with his family. With Mother anyway. Even better, their current chef might be the finest she had ever hired.

In the corner of the lab sat a steel bucket with a tight-fitting lid. Joran opened it and poured his failure into the fine sand inside. One of the first-year students would arrive later to empty the bin and clean up the equipment.

One of the best things about working at the college lab instead of a private business was the free cleaning service. In any other setting, he'd have to do it himself. Given some of the volatile substances he worked with, you couldn't just bring in some halfwit to dust and wash, not unless you wanted your lab and employee blown to bits.

The students all had enough training to handle the materials without being a danger to themselves or the building. They grumbled about the menial work, but they did it just the same. Joran had learned a great deal by paying attention to how the professors had set up their labs during his own cleaning days. Everyone had their preferences even though the students were all taught the same basic setup to start with.

Happily, his cleaning days were long past. He'd graduated two years ago and received the title of Grandmaster of Alchemy a year after that, at twenty-one, making him the youngest to earn the prestigious title. And despite what some of his detractors said, it wasn't a title you could buy. Only someone who devised a unique alchemical substance or process received it. Joran was one of only seventeen living.

You'd think that would be enough to satisfy his father, but you'd be wrong. He shook his head and started for the wooden double doors. Jorik Cade had still been a commoner at twenty-one, traveling right behind the imperial army, eager to trade with newly conquered people and reap the rewards from sales of exotic new items. He'd made his first fortune that way and Father believed his sons should follow in his footsteps.

For his part, Joran had no desire to thrash through jungles, fight off hostile natives and hungry beasts, or generally live the life of a frontier trader. He much preferred the controlled environment of his lab and the college. Pity Father refused to just agree to disagree.

Outside the lab, Joran took a deep breath of warm, humid summer air. The sweet perfume of thousands of blooming flowers brought a smile to his face. He'd processed all the local flowers in his first two years of study, extracting everything of value. Now he worked exclusively with items brought in from the farthest corners of the empire.

He turned left and made his way to the college's main campus. The shaded walkways, their roofs held up by massive white stone columns, kept the evening heat at bay. He walked alone, only the sound of his sandals slapping on the smooth stone path breaking the silence. The quiet gave him a chance to think, and today all that came to mind was how best to fend off his father's no doubt well-reasoned arguments for adventure.

"Joran!"

He turned to find the familiar figure of his best and perhaps only real friend, running toward him. Julian Mallus came from a common household and worked as an assistant librarian at the imperial library. A few inches shorter than Joran's modest five feet ten inches, Julian appeared younger than his true age of twenty-four. His short blond hair and blue eyes marked him as provincial rather than a true imperial. Mother wouldn't have approved of him hanging around with a provincial, which was one of the reasons Joran had never introduced his friend to the family.

Joran stopped to let the shorter man catch up. "Julian, library closed already?"

"Half an hour ago. Didn't you hear the temple ring five bells?"

Joran grimaced. In fact, he hadn't heard the huge bells at The One God's temple ringing out the hour. He'd been so focused he blocked everything else out.

"I hurried to catch you," Julian said. "There's going to be a vivisection at the arena tonight, do you want to go?"

"Who's performing it?" Joran asked.

"Primus Lucius from the Inquisition. They're using a prisoner from Oceanus, one of the ones that looks like a crab. When it's over I hear they might boil the body and give out samples."

Joran shivered at the mention of the Inquisition. Anyone, imperial or provincial, did well to fear those zealots. "Lucius is a butcher and just because you call performance torture vivisection doesn't make it science. No doubt he'll 'accidentally' use too little anesthetic just to hear the unlucky person's scream."

Julian looked left and right, the little muscle above his left eye twitching. "You shouldn't say that. What if someone heard you talking poorly about an inquisitor?"

"Then I'd point out one of the key articles of The One God's faith, 'Speak always the truth.'"

"Some truths are better spoken silently. I take it you don't want to join me?"

"No, thank you for the invitation. Even if a performance more appealing than Lucius carving some poor rebel into hors d'oeuvre was on offer, I'd have to pass. Tonight is my regular dinner with the family. Why don't you ask that girl you're always mooning over, the one that works in the kitchens?"

Julian reddened to his ears. "She's so pretty, I can't just walk up to her and ask. Can I?"

"Of course you can. Worst-case scenario, she says no and you watch the slaughter alone. If you keep hesitating, someone else will steal her out from under you."

His friend's face looked as red as Lucius's victim would after an hour in boiling water. Julian drew himself up. "Maybe I will. Yes! Tonight's the night. Thanks, Joran. Good luck with your father."

"I'll take all the luck I can get."

———

Jorik Den Cade read the income report from his newest trading post for the third time. No matter how many times he added up the numbers and even granting the most generous interpretations of his manager's letter, only one explanation existed: the little shit was skimming at least forty percent of the profits.

He crumpled up the letter and threw it across his office. The paper ended up on the floor in front of a leather and exotic hardwood chair Sestia had bought him for his birthday three years ago. It was a beautiful piece, but five minutes sitting in it made his ass fall asleep. He saved it for especially unwelcome visitors.

Jorik pushed away from his teak and rosewood desk and stood, his back popping and knees complaining. Some days he felt like a young man and others he felt every one of his sixty years. Of course, he'd walked or ridden across half the empire in his youth and the mileage showed. He smoothed his perfectly trimmed and oiled goatee and headed for the office door.

One good thing about his thief of a manager, it would give him the perfect excuse to get his youngest son out of the capital and off on a proper adventure.

As soon as he stepped out into the hall the scent of roasting meat and vegetables pulled him toward the kitchen. Tonight was their twice-monthly family dinner, though it would be a small gathering indeed with Titus away on business and Quintus The One God knew where, probably passed out in a ditch, knowing his worthless firstborn.

He rounded a corner and entered the dining room to find his lovely wife busy smoothing the napkin beside Joran's plate. Only three places tonight. Looked like Titus's wife and the grandkids wouldn't be coming either. Just as well, since when he told Joran what he had in mind, there would likely be an argument.

A playful swat on the backside drew a startled yelp from Sestia. Ten years his junior, the noblewoman looked every bit as beautiful as the day he married her. Sure, her dark hair had a few streaks of gray and there were a few more wrinkles around her eyes and mouth, but they only added to her beauty as they reminded Jorik of the wonderful memories they shared.

Sestia frowned at him. "I swear, Jorik, your manners haven't improved despite being a nobleman for thirty years."

Jorik grinned. "What is it the nobles like to say when they think I'm not listening? Ah, I remember: 'You can take the commoner out of the fields, but you can't take the fields out of the commoner.'"

She put her arms around his neck and kissed him. Familiar warmth filled him as he held her. How had he gotten so lucky?

He hated to spoil the happy feeling, but he needed to tell her what he had planned. "I'm going to send Joran south to deal with the manager trying to rob me blind."

Sestia stepped back and her frown deepened. "He won't like it. He might even refuse."

"No, no more refusing. That boy needs to get out of the city and see the world. There's more to life than his precious lab. He needs to learn that and the only way is in person. I intend to make that clear this time."

"He's a grown man, Jorik, and he can make his own choices, even if you don't like them."

"He's my son and I know what's best for him. Besides, there's no one else I can send."

"Joran Den Cade," the footman announced from the front door.

"You won't fight me on this, will you?" Jorik asked.

Sestia shook her head. "I won't, but your son is a Cade and every bit as stubborn as his father."

E very time the footman announced him, Joran felt ridiculous. This was his home and everyone knew him. But the servant had his job to do and the one time Joran pointed out that the announcement might not be needed, he'd gotten a look of reproof that suggested the footman feared for his job should he fail to let everyone on the estate know that the youngest son had arrived for dinner.

So he bore it and when the footman opened double doors tall and wide enough to let a loaded wagon enter with room to spare, he stepped through. Joran paused a moment to run his finger over the carved surface. How much had Father paid to get the exotic animals inlaid into the wood? He didn't know but suspected the sum would cover his lab's operating expenses for a month.

Inside the marble-tiled entry, he scrubbed his sandals on the stiff-bristled rug placed there for that purpose. When he looked up, he smiled to find his mother approaching, arms raised for a hug. She wore one of her favorite blue silk robes. He recognized the shade as Cade Cerulean. Joran had created the dye that produced it.

They embraced for a moment then Mother stepped back and put her hands on either side of his face. "So thin. You're not eating enough. And no mustache. I told you last time it was the style this year. Can't you at least try and keep up with current fashion?"

Joran swallowed a sigh. "I appreciate the concern, Mother, but as *I* said last time, in my line of work an oiled mustache is more likely to catch on fire than make a fashion statement, and I'd just as soon avoid burning my nose off."

She shook her head but released his face. "And no date? I

told you to feel free to bring any of your lady friends for dinner. If you got out more, you might even find your soulmate."

Joran had no lady friends, at least not the way Mother meant it. And finding his soulmate, wonderous as that would be, had nothing to do with love or romance. It literally meant finding the person that carried the other half of his soul. He worked, slept, and, if he remembered, ate something and got his daily hour of exercise. He had so much to learn that no time remained for romance. Besides, Titus had a wife and family and would no doubt inherit the business someday. Speaking of which…

He cocked his head. "I hear no screaming children. Titus and his family couldn't make it?"

"Your brother has gone north to negotiate with the dwarves." Father stood in the doorway that led to the dining room. He wore his preferred uniform of black trousers, white shirt, and black vest.

"Good evening, Father." Joran strode over to the old man and they shook hands.

Then they locked gazes and he feared the night's argument might begin before the meal came out. He really hoped not. Joran didn't want to walk out with an empty stomach.

"Camellia sent a note saying little Sextus wasn't feeling well and she didn't want to pass it along to one of us." Mother stepped between them, breaking some of the tension. "Let's sit down. Dinner will be ready soon."

"Should I brew a cure all?" Joran asked.

The cure all sat at the absolute peak of healing alchemy and did exactly what its name implied: cure any illness or injury. The only thing it couldn't heal was the passage of time and he suspected no one beyond The One God had the power to over-come that particular issue. The ruinous cost of the materials needed to brew it also made the potion too expensive for any but the richest families.

Joran let his mother lead him to his usual spot to Father's left. He sank into the soft cushion and his stomach rumbled, recognizing that meal time had arrived.

"No need for drastic measures." Mother sat opposite him and offered a faint smile. "It's just an upset stomach, he'll be fine in a day or two."

"It's important to force children to toughen up," Father said.

The unsubtle dig once would have set Joran's teeth on edge. Now he shrugged it off. He'd accepted that Father couldn't help himself. Mother's sharp look implied less understanding.

Once again, the inevitable argument got cut off by the arrival of a beautiful woman, or in this case four beautiful women. The serving girls each wore simple white cotton tunics that went to just above the knee and carried a platter of food. They all appeared to be Joran's age or younger with perfect figures, white hair, and slightly pointed ears. Half-ancient slaves were rare even in Tiber, and having four of them marked their family as among the richest. Not that anyone needed to see the slaves to realize the Den Cades' wealth.

One of the girls poured wine while the others served up plates of meat, vegetables, and soft white bread. Joran's mouth watered. The food's quality made bearing his father's annoying habits tolerable. The salves withdrew and the family all bowed their heads.

"We give thanks to The One God; the emperor, may he rule for a thousand years; and all those who came before us to build our magnificent empire." Mother spoke the standard pre-meal prayer softly but with obvious feeling. "In all their names we accept this meal. So say we all."

"So say we all," Joran murmured in time with his father.

Joran had met many members of The One God's priesthood during his time at college and the more of them he met, the less he believed in the general benevolence of their divine overseer. The gathering of wealth and political power seemed to interest most of them far more than doing good works.

Putting the hypocrisies of the priesthood out of his mind, he loaded a fork and ate. The savory mix of meat and vegetables filled him with joy. Even Father saw no need to speak as they devoured the scrumptious meal.

Far too soon the last bit of gravy had been sopped up and Father let out a contented belch. As if summoned by the noise, the slaves returned and cleared the table.

"A wonderful meal as always, Mother."

"Thank you, dear."

"Now that the meal is over," Father said. "We have matters to discuss."

And now Joran had to pay for his fine dinner. "Matters?"

"Indeed. The manager of my Stello Province trading post is stealing at least forty percent of the post's profits. I need you to go south to the provincial capital and get the matter straightened out. If I'm right, fire the manager and promote his assistant as a replacement. And if I'm wrong, well, I'm not wrong."

Father hadn't tried this approach yet. Likely the manager really was skimming the profits which meant someone had to be sent. Though that someone hardly needed to be him.

"Do you really think that's the best use of my time?" Joran asked. He'd try appealing to Father's greed. Sometimes that worked better than other strategies. "I'm close to perfecting the new perfume we discussed. You'll make fifty times whatever this manager is stealing when you sell it."

"The perfume will still be there when you return. We can't let someone get away with stealing from us."

Time to try a different angle of attack. "You've got a dozen senior managers, any one of which knows more about the business than I do. Send one of them and I can continue working on the new perfume."

"No. It must be one of the family. We have to show that they can't get anything over on us just because we're far from the provinces. My work here can't be delegated. Titus is in the north. Quintus…Quintus is Quintus and so of no use in this situation. That leaves you."

Joran shook his head. "Sorry, Father, but traveling to the ass end of the empire holds no appeal for me. Send a senior or wait for Titus to get home, I don't care, but I have no intention of going."

Father surged to his feet. "You are going and that's the end of it."

Joran stood as well, a bit more slowly given his full stomach. "I refuse."

"Then I'll pull your funding." Father jabbed a finger at him. "Never forget who pays for that lab of yours."

"If that's your decision, I understand." Father blinked at him as if not understanding. "I'm sure one of the other trading houses will be eager to finance my work. The profits from the new crimson dye should fund my research for years."

"You can't do that!" Father balled up his fists and for a moment Joran feared his father might actually take a swing at him. They'd had plenty of arguments over the years, but none of them had ever come to blows.

Mother finally stood and put a hand on each of their shoulders. Father relaxed at once.

She turned to Joran. "Won't you do this thing for your father? It would mean a lot to him to know that someone he trusts completely is handling the matter."

"One time only?" Joran asked. He couldn't believe he was even considering such a stupid thing.

"On my honor," Father said.

"I want it in writing along with a guarantee of my funding."

Father actually looked pained. "You don't trust my word?"

"I trust that you mean it right now, but in a year or maybe two, you'll decide that one more little adventure will be good for me and then we'll be right back here for another fight. A contract is the one thing I have total faith that you'll honor. As soon as I see a signed paper registered at the solicitors' guild, I'll be on my way."

"Fine." Father returned to his chair. "Have it your way."

Joran nodded once and turned toward the door. His fine meal felt like lead in his stomach. His arguments with Father always left him sick to his stomach, but this one had been especially bad. Even worse, now he'd have to actually go on one of Father's stupid adventures.

Mother walked with him to the door and they paused.

"Did you have to demand a contract?"

"Look me in the eye and tell me anything I said was wrong and I'll march right back in there to apologize."

She looked away. "You weren't wrong, but some things shouldn't be said out loud. You hurt him tonight."

Joran grimaced. "I didn't want to hurt him, but I'm weary of these arguments. I saw a chance to end them and I took it, for better or worse. Goodnight, Mother."

She stood on her tiptoes and kissed his forehead. "Sleep

well, Joran. And try not to fret. You may find the journey more pleasant than you fear."

Since it could hardly be worse, he didn't bother to argue. With any luck he'd make the trip in a month or so, get the trading post sorted out, and be home in time to enjoy the fall, from the warmth and comfort of his lab.

CHAPTER 2

The sun had only been up for an hour when a messenger boy showed up at Joran's door with the contract, signed by his father and sealed with the scale and quill symbol of the solicitors' guild. It showed the power wielded by the Den Cade family that Father got it done in twelve hours. In addition to the contract, the boy had a ticket for passage south on a coach departing at nine in the morning. He'd have just time enough to pack before setting out for the carriage yard.

Now Joran was lugging his portable alchemy kit over his left shoulder and a modest carryall with a few days' worth of clothes and other essentials in his right hand. He managed the steps down from his second-floor apartment with considerable muttering and cursing. But he refused to back down. Father had held up his end and he'd do the same. And after this trip, no more arguments or interruptions to his work.

He could hardly wait.

A personal servant to handle his luggage would have been nice, but he disliked having strangers in his home. Besides, the carriage yard waited only six blocks from his apartment building in Second Circle. Even though he spent most of his time in the lab, Joran made a point of exercising for an hour every morning. A strong body housed a strong mind, or so his mentor always claimed.

When he reached the bottom of the steps, he let out a grunt of relief. He turned toward the street and nearly ran right into Julian. The two men stared at each other and Joran wasn't certain who'd surprised whom the most.

"Joran," Julian said at last. "Are you going somewhere? I went to the lab and you weren't there so I feared you might have caught something."

"I did. Family obligations." Joran forced his carryall into Julian's empty hands. "Here, take that. You can walk me to the carriage yard."

They set out and Joran noted the huge smile creasing his friend's face. At least one of them seemed to have something good going on. "What's got you so happy?"

"She said yes."

Joran blinked in confusion. "Who said what now?"

"Catia, the girl from the kitchens. I took your advice and asked her to the vivisection last night. She said yes. We even had dinner afterward. She's so nice."

Charming, torture and a meal, certainly an unforgettable first date.

Out loud Joran said, "Congratulations. As for me, I'm headed south to Stello Province to sort out some business issues at one of the family trading posts. Most likely I'll be gone for at least three months. I'm pleased to hear you'll have someone to keep you company during my absence."

Julian stopped dead in the street forcing Joran to turn back. While Joran wouldn't have minded missing his coach and delaying his inevitable departure, Father might consider that a breach of the contract and he didn't want to risk it.

"What's the problem?"

"Stello Province is a war zone. I mean a literal, active war zone. The Fifth, Sixth, and Seventh legions led by the Iron Legion are trying to crush a native rebellion, but they can't come to grips with the enemy. The natives live in the dense jungle, hitting and running at will. They've even attacked the provincial capital a few times."

This was all news to Joran. "How do you know so much?"

"My favorite tavern is near a barracks and the soldiers like to come in and drink. They also like to gossip."

The tightness in his chest loosened a little. "So this is rumor, not fact?"

"The worry in the soldiers' voices sounded real enough. Be careful, Joran."

They set out again, keeping to the sidewalk and avoiding the many wagons carrying the supplies needed to keep a city the size of Tiber functioning.

Five minutes of walking saw them through the gate separating Second and First Circles and entering a round, open area with three coaches sitting on the cobblestones. Grooms tended horses and adjusted tack, drivers paced as if impatient to get going, and a trio of footmen dressed in brown tunics and tan trousers waited beside the carriage doors to greet the passengers.

One of the footmen spotted Joran and Julian. He hurried over and bowed. "My lords, how may we be of service?"

Joran handed over his ticket and after a moment of study the footman said, "You have a long journey ahead of you, my lord. Your coach departs in ten minutes. This way please."

They followed the footman to the left-hand carriage. The

driver already sat in his seat. Despite the heat he wore a long cloak and broadbrimmed hat. The footman took the bag from Julian and passed it up to the driver who added it to the heap of luggage already on the roof.

When the footman held out a hand for Joran's portable alchemy kit he shook his head. One look at the less-than-gentle treatment convinced him to keep the kit with him. He'd taken time to pad every slot and he used ultra-durable glass for just about everything not made of metal, but better safe than sorry.

"This is delicate equipment. I assume there's room for it under the seat?"

"Certainly, my lord, if that's your preference. Southern Coaches always strives to grant the requests of its passengers."

Joran handed over the case and watched as the footman carefully slid it under the forward-facing bench. Satisfied that his gear was as safe as possible under the circumstances, he turned back to Julian. His friend eyed the coach and gnawed a lip.

"Relax," Joran said. "When I get back, you'll have to introduce me to Catia. Maybe we can all have dinner together and I'll tell you about the savage south."

Julian gave a little shake and forced a smile. "Sure, Joran. Do you need me to do anything while you're gone?"

Joran thought for a moment then shook his head. He had no plants, no pets, no nothing beyond his work and books. Everything he owned would survive perfectly fine in his absence.

"I can't think of anything." Joran climbed up into the coach. "Take care, my friend."

Five minutes later four more people crowded into the coach and they were off. His unwelcome journey had begun.

CHAPTER 3

Joran had been fairly certain he'd hate traveling and a month on the road from sunup to sunset had done nothing to change his mind. The benches needed more padding than the inch of stuffing that covered them. Each day ended at an inn with a poor meal of mystery-meat stew and a straw-filled mattress. Only his complete exhaustion after getting rattled around for fourteen hours made the accommodations bearable. The poor driver had it even worse, having to tend the horses each night before enjoying his own meal.

But at last, they were almost to Cularo. One more night at an inn then tomorrow, late, they'd arrive at the provincial capital. And thank The One God for that. Since they entered Stello Province the road had gotten steadily worse. They left cobblestones behind two weeks ago and were now running on rutted dirt. When he mentioned the state of the road to the driver two nights ago, the man had smiled and said he should be glad it was the dry season. During the rainy season sometimes the roads grew impassible for weeks and the passengers were forced to stay at one of the inns.

He shuddered when he remembered the conversation. A week at one of the dreary little roadside inns and he'd set out on foot.

Sweat dripped down his face and he wiped it away. He'd once believed Tiber grew hot in the summer, but he hadn't known what hot was until now. Heavy leather shades covered the coach windows to keep out dust, but he raised the one nearest to him anyway. It had to be close to noon, and the air nearly suffocated him.

The woman across from him, Belena, let out a sigh as the warm breeze filled the coach. "The One God bless you, young man, that feels wonderful."

He smiled at being called "young man" by a woman at most five years his senior. Her sweat-soaked white robe clung to her ample figure. Dark eyes and hair marked her as an imperial, but he suspected she had common blood rather than noble. She and the little boy seated beside her had been his sole companions for the past ten days.

"The driver said I'll see my father tomorrow," the boy, Clodius, said. He had a grown-up way about him that reminded Joran of an older version of Sextus. He'd informed Joran in a serious voice that he would turn eight in twenty-three days. Thirteen days now.

"I know. Are you excited?"

"Oh, yes. Father promised in his last letter that he'd take my birthday off from the blacksmith shop and spend it with us."

Eight-year-old Joran would have been excited as well, but he didn't remember his father ever taking a whole day off to spend with his family, even their birthdays. Still, Joran had trouble believing anyone would send for their family given the state of things down here. The unrest seemed to be all they talked about at the inns.

Clodius surged out of his seat and crossed to the open window. "What is that?"

"I'm sorry if he's bothering you, my lord," Belena said.

"Not at all." Joran had nothing else to occupy him and the boy's antics helped the days pass a little faster.

He turned to look and his eyes widened in spite of himself. Perhaps a mile from the road, a huge red and gold ship suspended from an even larger balloon flew toward Cularo. A distinctive dragon-shaped figurehead gave the vessel its name. Joran had seen the massive flying ships a few times as they came and went from the imperial palace, but he never expected to see one this far from home. It must be carrying some important personnel. Generals or the like.

"That is an imperial dragon ship," Joran said. "Only the most powerful and important members of the court are allowed to travel in them. The journey that took us a month, they made in a week."

"Wow!"

Joran smiled. Wow, indeed.

They watched the ship grow closer by the second. When half a mile separated them, an explosion blew the side of the hull open and Joran swore he saw people go flying out along with crates and furniture. Shards of wood shot up into the balloon, ripping a huge hole and sending the whole thing crashing in slow motion into the jungle.

"Whoa!" the driver shouted as he brought the carriage to a halt.

"You two had best wait here," Joran said as he climbed out.

Clodius tried to follow but his mother wrapped him up and pulled him close. Thank The One God for that. He might have taken a shine to the boy, but he didn't need him underfoot just now.

The driver reached the ground a moment after Joran. "What should we do, my lord?"

As an imperial citizen, not to mention a trained alchemist and healer, Joran had an obligation to check and see if anyone lived through the crash. He grimaced at the jungle not ten feet from the rutted path they called a road. It would be a miserable walk, but the sooner he got started the sooner he could help anyone that needed it.

"I'm going to look for survivors. Take them to the inn and send help as quickly as you can."

"Yes, my lord." The driver hesitated then asked, "Do you think anyone survived that?"

"I don't know, but if there's any chance, I have to find out for sure. Hurry now."

Joran reached back to collect his bag.

"What's going on?" Belena asked.

"Don't worry, the driver will take you to the next inn." He offered the boy a reassuring smile and closed the door.

Now if someone would just offer him some reassurance.

The carriage clattered off and Joran paused long enough to open his bag and extract a half-full vial filled with clear liquid. He pulled the cork and applied a drop to each wrist and the back of his neck. That should keep the insects at bay for twelve hours. Maybe only ten if he sweat too much.

He replaced the vial and set out. Finding the crash site shouldn't be difficult—the stink of the burning hull reached him already. Forcing his way through some thick fronds and ducking under a vine, he made his way into the jungle.

Leaving aside the howling monkeys, shrieking birds, and oppressive heat, the walk was surprisingly peaceful. The uneven ground forced him to take his time lest he end up with a twisted ankle and need saving himself. A pleasant perfume from some unseen blossom filled the air. He'd have to ask the trading post people about the source. He could extract a fine perfume from it.

Fifteen minutes of hiking brought him to the wreckage. A line of broken wood covered the jungle. The keel had gouged an especially wide rut in the soft earth. The balloon ended up caught in the trees, forming a canopy that covered the bulk of the debris.

At least he could search in the shade.

Something exploded in what remained of the hull, sending a gout of bluish flames in the opposite direction from him. Joran knew that color of flame as well as anyone of his profession. A vial of alchemist's fire had exploded. The ship must have been carrying a load of weapons for the war effort. He doubted that had brought them down. Any quartermaster with even half a brain packed alchemist's fire in enough padding to survive even the clumsiest handling.

A flash of sunlight glinting off something caught his eye about ten feet from the hull. He hurried over and stared down at a dark-haired woman dressed in once-fine crimson robes. A gold amulet featuring a sword clutched in the claws of an eagle rested on her chest. Her bronze skin was covered with blood and bruises. That her chest still rose and fell defied belief.

Or maybe it was simple toughness. Everyone said the Iron Princess, Alexandra Tiberius, was tougher than any man under her command. Considering she commanded the entire imperial army, stood at most five feet four inches tall and had a petite build, that said something, mostly about the bards' powers of exaggeration.

Joran had seen her exactly twice before, both times at the

head of military parades in the capital. She hadn't looked like she was enjoying herself at the time, though he suspected she'd much prefer leading a parade to getting her dragon ship blown out of the sky.

He knelt, reached for her, and hesitated. Joran shook his head at his foolishness. No one would arrest him for trying to heal the princess.

Trying being the operative word. Just a casual glance revealed broken arms and legs, numerous shallow cuts and abrasions, and he had no idea what internal injuries. She needed a cure all, but he couldn't very well brew one here.

He rummaged through his kit and pulled out a vial filled with greenish crystals. He took a deep breath, pulled the cork, and waved it under her nose. Alexandra sputtered and coughed. No blood flecked her lips, so hopefully that meant no damage to her lungs. Thank The One God for small favors.

Her eyes opened, one perfectly undamaged and the other bloodshot and surrounded by a bruise that made it look like she'd lost a fist fight.

She focused on Joran. "Where am I and who are you?"

"My name is Joran Den Cade and you are approximately a day and a half north of Cularo which I assume was your destination. I happened to be looking out my carriage window when your dragon ship exploded."

Her thin, dark eyebrows drew down in a scowl. "I remember the explosion, but nothing after that. Were there other survivors?"

"I haven't checked the rest of the wreckage, but I'm not optimistic. In truth, it's a wonder you're alive, given the state of your body."

"Why can't I move my arms and legs?"

"Likely because you've severed your spinal cord. I need to

find something to stabilize your neck, so you don't do any more damage. Hopefully the coach driver will reach the nearest inn soon and they'll dispatch help. Though I doubt it will arrive before morning."

"That is less than ideal." Alexandra's gaze had shifted to somewhere over his right shoulder.

Joran slipped the green crystals back into his kit and pulled out a different vial along with a packet of pills. He stood slowly and turned. Facing him were six of the locals, their mottled green scales blending so perfectly with the jungle that some of their bodies seemed to disappear. What remained perfectly clear were the stone-tipped spears they held leveled at Joran and Alexandra.

Did they even speak Imperial? Joran doubted it and didn't want to take his eyes off them to find a translation potion. He'd heard nothing about local allies. In fact, he'd heard no details of any sort regarding the natives. Best to assume any he encountered were hostile. Still, better to try and avoid a fight with the princess so close and in such bad shape.

"Greetings," Joran said. "We are most grateful that you came to offer assistance."

They stared at him, yellow eyes blinking, seeming completely unaware of or uninterested in what he'd just said.

"Don't waste your breath," Alexandra said. "The savages can't speak a civilized tongue."

The lizardmen advanced a step and Joran made his decision.

He hurled the vial at the closest enemy.

When it shattered, a black cloud billowed out.

Not much time now.

He dropped to the ground beside Alexandra and shook out one of the pills. "Open your mouth, Princess. Quickly."

To her credit she asked no questions and opened her mouth an inch. He popped the pill onto her tongue and took one for himself a moment before the black cloud washed over them.

Joran saw nothing as the darkness surrounded them and heard only the tortured hisses and shrieks of the dying lizard-men. Thirty seconds later the mist dissipated, revealing the twisted bodies of the natives.

"What was that?" Alexandra asked.

"Dread spores." Joran stood again. "Very effective and with a common antidote. I always carry two vials for personal defense. Unfortunately, I gave you my second antidote, so I can't use it again. Do you think this bunch has friends?"

"I'd count on it. And if they're here, they're probably looking for the ship and any survivors. We will likely have more company soon. I don't suppose you have any more weapons in your bag of tricks?"

"I have some alchemist's fire, a couple vials of acid, and some paralyzing powder. I'd just as soon not use anything explosive lest I start a chain reaction with the supplies in your hold and blow us both to an early meeting with The One God."

"If it's that or letting the lizardmen kill us, I assure you, blowing up will be the less painful option."

CHAPTER 4

Mia Amino ran through the jungle, her bronze skin glistening with sweat. She'd left her stiff leather armor back at the castle, figuring speed and stealth would serve her better on this mission. Her silver-trimmed crimson tunic marked her as a member of the Iron Guard and any soldier that saw it would give Mia no trouble. Her Majesty's dragon ship should be passing overhead anytime now. So far Mia had seen no sign of hostile natives, thank The One God.

She'd left Cularo a little over a day ago to make sure the final leg of the princess's journey would be secure. The generals laughed when she suggested the precaution. None of the weapons employed by the local primitives had a hope of harming one of their dragon ships, they said. When she insisted, they welcomed her to go on her own, but made it clear no one else would be wasted on a fool's errand.

In her two years as a member of Alexandra's personal guard, Mia had gotten used to such dismissals. They considered her too young and inexperienced even as they acknowledged her fighting skills. They also considered her too common. Every other member of the Iron Guard had not only at least ten years of combat experience but a name that opened doors wherever they went. An orphan plucked out of the Tiber City Watch based solely on her ability probably struck them all as some passing fancy of the princess's. Mia had to make sure that she did nothing to make her patron regret taking a chance on her.

She paused and shaded her eyes to study a patch of sky through a gap in the canopy. Any moment now she expected to see the ship.

A moment later an explosion rattled the jungle. She spotted smoke a little to her left, close enough to the ship's path to make her stomach clench. The natives had nothing that might cause an explosion, that meant it must have been Alexandra's ship.

If anything happened to the princess...

She put the thought out of her mind, turned toward the smoke, and ran for all she was worth, stealth forgotten.

A quarter mile later a feeling of fear and determination unlike anything she'd ever experienced ran through her. It came from outside of her. She'd heard tales of the natives' demon magic, but never about spells like this. The feeling didn't frighten her so much as spur her on to move even faster. She must be picking up the princess's emotions. How such a thing might happen she had no idea, but nothing else made sense.

As soon as the powerful emotion came it vanished. Had Mia been less confident in herself, she might have thought she imagined the whole thing.

Half an hour of hard running brought her within sight of the ruined dragon ship. The hull burned and smoke filled the sky. Nothing could have survived a crash like that. Mia nearly collapsed in tears before another emotion slammed into her. Desperation this time. Someone must have survived and the only person she felt close enough to that she might sense their emotions was the princess.

Either that or she really was going mad.

One way or the other, she carried on. A few strides later she rounded a broken chunk of hull in time to see a man she didn't recognize doing something to the princess.

Mia didn't think beyond seeing that.

She drew her sword and rushed forward. No one would harm Alexandra while she had breath in her body.

He looked up as she approached and their eyes locked. A vibration ran through her whole body and an overwhelming desire to put her sword away filled her. Had he used some spell on her?

Mia fought the desire and slowed. "Step away from the princess if you wish to continue breathing."

"Her spine is severed," the man said. "If I don't finish bracing her neck and head, the slightest jolt could kill her. Where's the rest of the rescue team?"

Again the overwhelming desire to put her sword away washed over her and again she fought it down. "What rescue team? Who are you?"

He had no chance to answer before Alexandra said, "Put that sword away, Mia, you're making a fool of yourself. Don't you know a healer when you see one?"

"Try not to speak, Majesty," the man said. "I need you to keep your head still."

He had sticks and strips of cloth tied around Alexandra's forehead and neck as well as wrapped around her chest. Mia slipped her sword into its sheath.

"I sent my coach driver ahead to the nearest inn to fetch assistance. This seemed far too soon for it to arrive, but I did hope. Still, some help is better than none." He tied a final strip of cloth in place.

Mia took a step closer and the vibration grew so strong she feared she might explode. The strange man stared at her with wide eyes.

"Unbelievable, to think that I'd find you here." She had no idea what he meant, then he said, "You're my soulmate."

Mia nearly collapsed. Her soulmate. This man, in this place, carried the second half of her soul and she his? It seemed impossible and at the same time nothing else made sense.

Something hissed, breaking the spell.

Six natives emerged from the jungle, their stone spears at the ready.

"Take my hand, quickly," he said.

Mia hesitated. If they completed the bond, there was no going back. Her life would be different forever. She'd heard many stories about people finding their soulmates. No one had ever refused and no one had ever regretted the decision. The stories agreed on little else, but all agreed on that.

She took the final step and grasped his hand.

It felt like lightning ran through her body. Like something she didn't even know she lacked had appeared.

One of the lizardmen threw its spear.

The weapon seemed to fly in slow motion.

Mia drew her sword and cut it out of the air.

In the blink of an eye she closed with the natives, her sword a blur of imperial steel. The edge, hardened by alchemy, cut as easily through the natives' scales as it did the wood of their spears.

In ten heartbeats they lay in pieces on the ground. Mia

knew what she could do and this exceeded her normal abilities by many orders of magnitude.

"Very impressive," the man said. Warmth flooded through her at his pleasure and approval. "My name is Joran Den Cade and it is a pleasure to meet you, Mia."

———

Joran had long been fascinated by the phenomenon known as soul bonding. As he stared at his soulmate, he shook his head. What were the odds he'd even find his soulmate, much less that he'd do so in this horrid place? Mia stood over the bodies of the lizardmen she'd killed, gaping in wonder. Not at all surprising considering she'd just killed six armed opponents in less time than it would have taken Joran to describe the scene.

Still, best they got moving before even more of the natives showed up.

"I've stabilized your neck as well as I can, Majesty. If you'll excuse me, we need to build a stretcher so we can carry you out of here."

"Do what you must," Alexandra said. "I'm not going anywhere."

Nice that she retained her sense of humor. He moved closer to the ship and Mia joined him. "What happens now?"

"I'm looking for materials to build a stretcher. I'd hoped to wait for help, but with all the lizardmen in the area, that's asking for trouble even with your enhanced abilities."

"That's one of the things I wanted to ask about. How did I do what I did? It felt like the lizardmen were stuck in thick mud. Do you understand what's happening?"

"I understand the theory." Joran spotted a spear shaft

jutting up out of the rubble and yanked it out. Unfortunately it had snapped off halfway. He tossed it aside. "According to the books I've read, everyone is born with only half their soul. Somewhere else in the world, another person is born at the exact same moment with the other half. The vast majority of people go their entire lives without ever finding their soul-mate. The lucky few that do, gain access to the other half of their soul which gives them enhanced abilities."

"Like moving really fast?"

"Among other things. As a warrior, you naturally received physical enhancements: strength, speed, perception. For me, I find my mind has never been more clear. I suspect that any problem I applied myself to would be quickly solved. The potential is astonishing." Joran pointed at a section of balloon that had reached the ground. "Would you be so kind as to cut a section out of that large enough for the princess to lie on?"

She did as he asked and as expected imperial steel made short work of the thick material. Joran's own search ended when he found a pair of undamaged spears, their heads still gleaming despite the crash.

Mia hacked the spearheads off. "It can't be that simple. Nothing in life is free."

"True." Joran knelt and they worked together to assemble the stretcher. He hardly had to speak. It felt like she knew exactly what he needed her to do before he did. "There's a limit to the gift. Each soul-bonded pair is different, but I've never read about a pairing with a range greater than a quarter mile and most are considerably less. Outside of that range, instead of being twice as strong, you'll be half as strong. I suspect my mind will grow cloudy and unfocused. We'll both desire nothing so much as to be back within range of the other. There."

They'd built a passable stretcher, hopefully good enough to get Alexandra to the nearest inn.

Mia's enhanced strength allowed them to maneuver Alexandra onto the stretcher with minimal jarring to her damaged body. When they finished, Joran lifted the end with her feet and Mia took the end by her head.

"Let's make for the road," Joran said. "It'll be faster walking plus we might be able to see any lizardmen coming."

Mia didn't argue and they set out through the jungle. Though he held out little hope of finding any more survivors, Joran wished he could've taken one final look around the wreck to make sure he didn't miss anyone. But he didn't dare linger. Saving Princess Alexandra took priority over everything.

Ten minutes of steady walking brought them to the trade road. Perhaps Joran's strength had gotten a boost as well since he felt no need for a rest. Just as well since he doubted Mia had any intention of giving him one until Alexandra was safe.

Joran glanced at the shadows. They were getting longer by the minute. Hopefully they could reach the inn before full darkness set in.

"How did you find us so quickly, Mia?" Alexandra asked.

"I feared the natives might have laid a trap for your dragon ship, so I suggested scouting the route near Cularo. The raiders have been especially active over the last few weeks after all. The generals all laughed at me, but I went anyway. Better safe than sorry."

"Lucky for us," Joran said.

"You did well for a civilian," Alexandra said to him. "I'd certainly be dead right now if not for your timely arrival."

"I only did my duty as an imperial citizen, Majesty." A bolt of anxiety from Mia brought Joran up short. "What is it?"

"There's something up ahead in the road. I can't see what since most of it is around the corner."

"Let's set Her Majesty down and you can go take a look." Mia's reluctance came through their link. "I'll stay with her. Of the two of us, you're certainly the best suited for a scouting mission."

"With your permission, Majesty?" she asked.

"Go," Alexandra said.

They set the stretcher down and Mia hurried off out of sight around the bend. Joran shook his aching arms then knelt to check the binding holding Alexandra's head still. He tightened a few knots but for the most part they remained exactly as he put them.

"You realize that in saving my life, your own life has changed forever," Alexandra said. "Every member of the imperial court as well as the army will want to know your politics and how much sway you have over me. You're a noble, so that will help some. Don't think me ungrateful, but I need another complication in my life like I need a hole in the head."

"I hadn't given the politics of my decision any thought. As a healer, my duty was clear. Just out of curiosity, how much sway do I have over you?"

Despite her condition Alexandra managed a weak smile. "None whatsoever. But that won't stop the greedy, the arrogant, and the stupid from thinking otherwise."

"Frankly, Majesty, my greater concern is how Mia and I will manage our new situation. Apart, we'll be largely useless, but I can't imagine her being content to hang around the lab while I work and I certainly have no desire to join the Iron Guard."

"Let's focus on getting somewhere safe, then we'll figure out the rest."

Mia came jogging back around the corner. "Looks like the natives attacked a carriage. We've got three civilian casualties. They dragged the horses into the jungle, but I didn't follow."

Joran tried to squash the pain and failed. He hadn't known any of his traveling companions for long, but he'd liked them well enough. They certainly deserved better than to die on the side of the road in this forsaken corner of the empire.

Mia looked at him, her expression troubled. "Are you okay?"

"That was my carriage. The little boy, Clodius, reminded me of my nephew. He had a birthday coming up and was going with his mother to join his father in Cularo. I didn't even get their family name, so I can't tell his father that his family was killed. Hopefully I can get it from the coach company." Joran gave a shake of his head and bent to pick up the stretcher. "There's nothing to be done now and we have more pressing concerns."

Mia gave him one last searching look, picked up her end of the stretcher, and they set out. When they passed the carriage, Joran did his best not to look too closely at the ruined transport. The luggage had been ripped open and pawed through. He left it, not wanting anything the lizardmen had touched.

He needed to focus on the problem in front of him not what might have been. What happened here was completely out of his control.

He'd made the best decisions possible at the time. Now he had to live with them.

CHAPTER 5

Joran never would have imagined the sight of one of the dingy little roadside inns filling him with such joy. The inn, really more of a fort with food, a stable, and rooms for the guests, had two stories, narrow windows that doubled as arrow slits, and four guards armed with crossbows patrolling the perimeter. As soon as complete darkness settled in, they'd retreat back inside and the doors would be barred until sunrise.

The One God must have been watching over them, as they arrived with minutes to spare. A guard noticed them and loosed a shrill whistle. A shot of Mia's anxiety washed over Joran.

"Don't worry," he said. "We don't have scales, so I doubt they'll shoot us on sight.

The other three guards came jogging from every direction. One of them carried a lit lantern that spread a warm glow across the yard. The guards stopped when they got close. None of them bothered to raise their crossbows, confirming Joran's theory that only nonhumans approaching the inn would have trouble.

"What happened?" the guard with the lantern asked. "The coach is several hours overdue."

"Lizardmen attacked," Mia said. "We have a badly injured woman and require a room."

Good, she hadn't told the guards exactly who they had with them. Better to keep the princess's identity a secret for now. Not that Joran didn't trust the inn workers, but why take unnecessary risks?

The group made their way toward the front door, a heavy hardwood model that looked strong enough to stand up to a battering ram.

The lantern bearer opened the door and waved them through. "Come on, boys. We're calling it a day. With them scaly bastards on the rampage, we won't be seeing anyone else tonight."

Once everyone cleared the entrance, a different guard slammed the door tight and dropped a four-inch-thick beam into a pair of heavy steel brackets nailed into the wall. Joran blew out a breath. How long had it been since he felt safe?

Seemed like forever.

The noise drew a middle-aged woman out from the kitchen. She wore a simple tan tunic with an apron over it. A gaunt face and deep wrinkles gave testament to a hard life. Short, sandy hair marked her as a provincial.

Joran noticed the scent of cooking stew. His mouth watered, but he forced himself to focus. He needed to get somewhere out of the way and get the cure all going.

"What's all this?" the woman asked.

"Lizards hit the coach," the lantern bearer said.

"We need a room," Joran said. "Preferably before my arms fall off."

"Right, follow me." The woman led them to a set of steps leading to the second floor. "We've got plenty of space if the coach isn't coming. Name's Kora and I run this inn. I'm a fair hand at healing if you want me to take a look at the lady."

"Thank you for your kindness, ma'am," Joran said. "But I'm a trained healer and now that I have somewhere to work, I should be able to handle the injuries myself. I promise to call on you should I need help."

"You've got better manners than most of my imperial guests." Kora stopped at the first door and pushed it open. "Here you go. Good luck."

They marched in and Kora shut the door behind them. The room looked exactly like every room he'd stayed in since leaving Tiber. Two single beds with thin straw mattresses, a table and chair, and a chamber pot.

They set the stretcher down and Mia said, "Her Majesty can't stay in a room like this. It's beneath her dignity."

"My dignity can survive a lot worse than this."

Joran ignored the pair and set his case on the table. He had the reagents for a cure all, but his limited equipment would make the preparation a challenge. He set up the oil burner and placed a flask on a little tripod over it. A small mortar and pestle came out next; he'd need that in a moment.

"Do you prefer a quick cure or a slow cure, Majesty?" Joran asked.

"Quick. I haven't the time for a three-day nap."

He adjusted his plans according to her wishes. "It will be quite painful you understand."

"Majesty, maybe you should take the slow cure," Mia said. "You've suffered enough as it is."

"If I leave those morons in charge of the war for three extra days, The One God alone knows what else they might screw up. No, the sooner we get to Cularo, the better. Prepare the quick cure."

"Yes, Majesty." Joran lit the burner and selected a vial filled with filtered troll's blood. He needed to reduce its volume by half before he added the next ingredient.

"You are qualified to brew a cure all, right?" Alexandra asked.

"I'm a master healer and a grand master alchemist. Rest assured, this is far from the first cure all I've prepared."

He watched the now-bubbling liquid carefully; the next ingredient had to go in at precisely the right moment. If he screwed this step up they were done. He only had the one vial of blood. Not that he thought he was going to. His hands had never been so steady or his mind so clear. A gift of the soul bond he felt certain.

Half an hour later he removed the completed potion from the heat and set it in a metal holder. "Now we need to let it cool."

"What is a grand master alchemist doing in Stello Province?" Alexandra asked.

"Family business. My father asked me to look into some troubles he's been having at his trading post in Cularo. Normally my elder brother would handle this sort of thing, but he's off on other business, so here I am. Since I met my soulmate, perhaps the journey was fated."

"Or perhaps it's the luck of the Tiberius family. I suspect if anyone else had been on that coach, I'd be dead right now." Alexandra coughed and cleared her throat.

Mia hurried over. "Are you okay, Majesty?"

"I'm as fine as possible given my circumstances. Though I

fear I may have trouble swallowing that potion."

"You won't have to." Joran touched the vial and found it still too hot. "A cure all is designed to be absorbed through your saliva glands. Oftentimes a person in need of one is either unconscious or otherwise unable to swallow."

"Good to know. Mia, why don't you go down and get some food for you and Joran."

"I shouldn't leave you, Majesty."

"Woman, you hover worse than my nanny when I was three."

Mia looked at Joran who tried to project feelings of reassurance. "I need a bite to eat and so do you. Don't worry, I'll keep a close watch on her."

Her stomach growled loud enough for them all to hear and her face flushed. "Fine, I'll be right back."

When the door closed and her footsteps vanished Joran said, "She's very devoted."

"Too devoted. Don't get me wrong, I demand loyalty from all my people, but Mia takes it too far. She's obsessed."

Joran's eyes widened as he finally understood the strange mix of emotions that had been bouncing around in his head. "Not obsessed, in love. She's in love with you."

"How...? Oh, right, soul bound. That would certainly explain her behavior. It's fortunate for both of us that you arrived when you did. Much as it would have pained me, I intended to remove her from the Iron Guard as soon as the campaign in Stello ended. Her constant fussing makes it nearly impossible at times for me to do my job."

"How, exactly, does my arrival help with that?" Joran checked the potion again. Nearly ready.

"You're soulmates. Her infatuation will transfer from me to you. Then I'll be free of her hovering and constant worry.

Hopefully it will also allow her to do her job with a clear head. Though I may have to make arrangements for you to join me, perhaps as an advisor or something."

Joran nearly choked, both on the idea that Mia's feelings for Alexandra would transfer to him and that he would have to join her retinue. Neither appealed to him and one was likely impossible. He debated how best to tell the third-most-powerful person in the empire all that until Mia returned with two plates covered with stew and rolls. That awkward conversation would have to wait. Besides, the potion had finished cooling.

"If you like, you can set those on the table and we can eat while the healing process begins. Let me give her the potion and I'll clean up my mess."

Mia obliged, barely taking her eyes off of Alexandra as she did. Poor girl really had it bad. He picked up the now-cooled cure all and carried it over to Alexandra.

He knelt beside her head and she asked, "How long?"

"Given the state of your body, twelve hours at minimum. Open your mouth as wide as you can, please."

She did so, giving him a target about an inch across. Plenty big enough, thank The One God. He really didn't want to have to force her mouth wider, not with Mia's giant ball of worry lodged in his brain. Who knew what she might have done if he'd had to pry Alexandra's jaws open.

A trickle at a time, Joran poured the cure all into her mouth until he'd emptied the vial.

"I feel nothing," said Alexandra.

"It takes half a minute to begin working. That's to give you a chance to get the whole dose down."

"Oh...AHHH!" Her jaw clenched hard and her muscles spasmed.

Mia appeared beside him, her concern hitting him like a truncheon. "What's wrong with her?"

"Nothing." Joran straightened. "As I said, the short cure is painful. Right now the potion is doing exactly what it's supposed to."

He spent a few minutes cleaning his equipment with the towel he kept in his kit for that purpose. Once they reached real civilization, he'd have to do a more thorough job, but for now at least nothing would leak and contaminate his other supplies.

That done, he tossed the now-stained towel onto one of the beds and sat. He pushed one plate to the far side of the table and pulled the other to him. "Won't you join me? There's nothing you can do for her until the potion wears off. Her Majesty isn't even aware of your presence."

Mia shot him a hard look. "She might be."

Time to try another tactic. "If you faint from lack of food, how will you protect her?"

She looked from him to Alexandra, indecision warring within her. Finally, she joined him at the table. They ate in silence for a few minutes before she said, "I know it annoys Her Majesty when I fuss, but I can't seem to help myself. Some of the other members of the Iron Guard laugh at me, when they think I can't hear."

Should he broach the subject? Despite their bond, he really knew nothing about Mia.

Oh well, now was as good a time as any to learn.

"I understand that unrequited love can be difficult, especially when the one you love is so far above you socially."

"Love!" The word came out as a shriek. "How did you...? I mean, I never said anything. Did Her Majesty tell you?"

Joran tapped the side of his head. "Our emotions are linked.

What you feel, I feel and vice versa. Of course, given what a bundle of nerves you've been since we met, I suspect little enough of my feelings are getting through. It took me a while to sort them out. Some things the princess said helped."

Mia nearly dropped her fork halfway to her mouth. "She spoke to you about me? What did she say?"

Joran couldn't lie to her, the bond wouldn't allow it. He debated refusing to answer, but Mia needed to know and the sooner the better.

"She said she was relieved we formed a soul bond. It seems she believes that our link will divert your emotions from her to me." Joran licked his lips. Now the hard part. "She also said she'd been considering removing you from the Iron Guard."

A strangled gasp slipped from between Mia's lips. "She wishes to be rid of me?"

"Not you, but the constant pressure your feelings put on her. I believe she respects you as a warrior, but that's the extent of her interest." Pain and sorrow washed over him with such force that he nearly broke into tears. Forcing himself to focus through the powerful emotions, he continued. "I don't tell you this to cause you pain. But if you wish to remain in her service, you must keep yourself under control."

Mia wiped her eyes. "Will my emotions transfer from her to you now that we're bonded?"

Joran finished his dinner and set his fork on the pewter plate. "I don't think so, though every soul bond is different. Contrary to what many people believe, finding a soulmate has nothing to do with love or sex. Often a soulmate is the same sex."

"What's wrong with that?" Mia demanded.

Joran massaged the bridge of his nose. This really wasn't going as well as he'd hoped.

"There's nothing wrong with it. My point is, the soul bond is a unique relationship. Plenty of soul bonded wed others and have a family with someone other than their soulmate. I've even read about instances where different species have formed soul bonds. One had a human and dwarf pair." He shook his head at the unpleasant memory. "That turned out to be an absolute tragedy. The human half died at seventy-five while the dwarf still had hundreds of years left. She committed suicide a month after he died, apparently unable to bear the loss."

Mia stared at him. "Why would The One God create such a pairing if it had to end in tragedy?"

Joran held his hands out to the side. "Why did he let you fall in love with the princess when nothing could ever come from it? I'm an alchemist. I understand what I can see and touch. Dealing with the whys and hows of love is far outside my expertise."

"What am I going to do?" Mia asked.

Joran reached over and took her hand. With all his will he pushed faith and reassurance through their link. "Whatever happens, I promise we'll deal with it together."

CHAPTER 6

Silence woke Joran from a deep sleep. He'd gotten so used to Alexandra's groaning and thrashing that their absence jarred him. When he sat up he found Mia already at her side cutting away the bindings holding her to the stretcher. A mixture of exhaustion and relief filled his soulmate. It felt like she hadn't gotten any sleep last night. No doubt too worried about the princess.

He rolled out of bed and stretched his aching shoulders. Between carrying the stretcher and sleeping on an inch-thick straw mattress, everything had started to ache. He had a pill in his kit that would get rid of the discomfort in an instant, but he preferred not to rely on his own cures save in emergencies.

"How are you feeling, Majesty?"

Mia cut the last strip of cloth and Alexandra sat up. "Starving, but otherwise everything appears functional. Your potion even repaired a nasty crick in my knee that I've been fighting for a month. Now that my mind's clear, I finally remember why your name sounded so familiar. You're Jorik's youngest son."

"Yes, Majesty. Though he never mentioned making your acquaintance."

"Oh, we've never met in person."

Alexandra stood and stretched, pulling the cloth of her torn robe tight across her chest. Her short, dark hair complemented her delicate bone structure. Now that the bruises were gone and he didn't fear for her life, Joran took a moment to appreciate just how lovely the princess looked despite the desperate need for a bath.

A flash of jealousy drew his attention to Mia who pierced him with a glare. Right, looking too closely at his soulmate's love interest was probably rude, even if the feelings weren't mutual.

"Your family is prominent enough that the scribes keep a file on you in the palace." Alexandra offered a wan smile. "Father insisted that my brother and I memorize all of them. The Den Cades are the richest family in the empire."

Joran smiled back. "Perhaps after the Tiberius family."

She laughed. "You have me there. First breakfast, then a bath, then we need to get to Cularo as quickly as possible."

"Do you wish to eat here or in the common room, Majesty?" Mia asked.

"Here. I'm in no fit state to see anyone. Pity my wardrobe ended up burned to a crisp."

"You got dinner so it's only fair that I get breakfast." Joran took a step toward the door.

"No," Alexandra said. "I wish to speak with you. Mia, you get the food."

Mia bowed. "Yes, Majesty."

Her annoyance poked Joran before Mia slipped silently out of the room. Joran would have given a great deal to be back home in his lab right now. Instead, he found Alexandra eyeing him the way a cat might a mouse.

"It seems her infatuation hasn't dimmed yet."

"No, Majesty. I spoke with her about the situation while you were healing. Even after I explained that you didn't feel about her the way she did about you and that her behavior endangered her position in the Iron Guard, I didn't get the impression that anything would change, especially in her heart. As for the soul bond, it doesn't alter the emotions of the bonded pair. That is to say, Mia isn't going to fall in love with me just because of the link."

If Alexandra's smile had been charming, her frown terrified him. "In that case, I have no choice but to remove her. Unless, of course, another arrangement can be reached."

Joran didn't like the sound of that at all. "What sort of arrangement?"

"I've been looking for an alchemist to serve as my advisor. The youngest grand master in history would fill the role perfectly. You're also a nobleman, which should keep the complaints to a minimum. Of course, as my personal advisor, you'd be far too important to not have your own dedicated bodyguard."

So Joran either agreed to completely upend his life or Mia would be banished from the sight of the person she loved most. That would likely destroy her and the thought of her pain tore at him. He found the idea of Mia suffering nearly unbearable. He could see now just how difficult a soul bond would make his life. Not that anything besides death had the power to sever that link. Even worse, his heart raced at the mere notion of losing it.

"I have family business to deal with in Cularo," Joran said. "When it's done, I'll join your service. Fair enough?"

"As long as you take her with you when you go, yes, it's fine." Alexandra's smile returned. "I'm sure having you by my side will make my work go more smoothly. Military alchemists tend to have a very narrow worldview. Having a new pair of eyes can only help."

"I'll do my best, of course, but my knowledge of military tactics are limited at best."

She waved him off. "I need no one's help when it comes to tactics. Father didn't grant me full command of the army simply because I'm his daughter. My weakness lies in more esoteric knowledge. Alchemy certainly, as well as whatever weird magic our many enemies wield."

The door opened and Mia entered carrying a laden tray. The food matched the room, cheap and bland. That said, oatmeal with ham bits and rolls certainly filled you up. They sat around the table, Alexandra making certain Joran stayed between her and Mia, and dispatched their breakfast with a minimum of conversation.

When they finished the meal Alexandra once more dispatched Mia, this time to collect hot water and a cloth for her bath. When she returned Mia asked, "Do you require assistance, Majesty?"

Joran couldn't believe she'd even asked that given everything he told her earlier.

"I certainly do not. Both of you, out in the hall."

Mia stared at the closed door clearly wishing for it to turn invisible. He had no potion for that, luckily for all of them.

Finally she turned on him and in a fierce whisper asked, "Why were you flirting with Her Majesty?"

Joran stared at her for a second. "I wasn't flirting with her."

"You were. I've never seen her smile and laugh and tease

with anyone like that. She usually just barks orders and argues with the generals."

"Have you ever seen her with other nobles?"

Now Mia stared at him. "The generals are nobles as well."

"The military is its own organization. The nobility is separate and unique, though not necessarily in a good way. When nobles meet for the first time, they have a way of acting as they get a feel for each other. Where they stand, what they think, that sort of thing. The teasing and fake laugh are part of it. When women do it, you might mistake it for flirting. I assure you there's no honest emotion behind her smiles."

"If it's all fake, how do you know what another noble is thinking?"

"You don't." Joran tried and failed to hide the disgust in his voice. "That's the point. They'll smile and laugh all while looking for the best place to stick a knife. The princess was raised at court surrounded by this nonsense. I can well understand her eagerness to focus on the military."

"You talk about the nobility as if you aren't a part of it." Alexandra splashed something prompting Mia to lick her lips.

"Hey. You need to stop thinking about her that way. A husband will be chosen for her by her father when it's most advantageous for the imperial family. Frankly, I'm surprised it hasn't happened already. Perhaps because her brother already has a wife and two potential heirs. The point is, there's no future where you and the princess are anything more than master and servant. But I did make a deal to allow you to stay close to her, assuming you can keep your lust under control."

Mia forced her gaze away from the door. He'd expected her to be angry, but she looked more confused. "You made a deal?"

He nodded. "She wants me to serve as her advisor on alchemical and magical matters. She said you'll be assigned to act as my bodyguard. Since I'll be close to her and you'll be close to me, well, you get the idea."

Her lips turned down a fraction and her confusion grew. "You seem unhappy. Serving as a close advisor to a member of the imperial family is a great honor."

"No doubt about that, assuming you're interested in court politics and increasing your personal standing. All I want is to do my research and work in the lab. Like as not my researching days are over."

"Then why did you agree?"

"Because if I didn't, she would have kicked you out of the Iron Guard and no doubt banished you as far from her side as possible."

Mia's face twisted and her pain struck him like a physical blow. If just hearing about it did that to her, the reality would've been ten times worse.

"I couldn't let that happen to you. We're soul bound. What hurts you, hurts me. What you want, I want for you, even though in this case all the wanting in the world won't make it happen. I protect you, you protect me. That's what it means to be bound."

A final splash preceded the door opening. A clean if still roughly dressed Alexandra stood in the entrance. "Well, I'm reasonably human again. Let's see about getting some horses."

"The stable will have a team of carriage horses," Joran said. "Saddles might be a problem."

Alexandra waved a hand and winked at him. "I've ridden bareback plenty of times."

That was definitely flirting. At least Mia's jealousy didn't stab him again.

Joran collected his alchemy kit and they went downstairs. Kora stood behind the bar. The guards must have gone out to begin their daily patrol. Alexandra strode right up to the bar, every inch the princess despite her torn, ragged clothes.

"We need three horses," Alexandra said.

"The carriage horses belong to the company. I can't sell them, sorry."

"I wasn't offering to buy them. My name is Alexandra Tiberius and as a member of the imperial family, I'm taking three horses to Cularo. Don't worry, I'll have some of my men return them when we arrive."

Alexandra swept toward the door with Mia a step behind. Joran slipped Kora a pair of gold imperials and shrugged as if to say, "What can you do?"

Joran had learned the hard way that the answer, when dealing with a member of the imperial family, was nothing.

———

While Her Majesty may have ridden bareback before, Mia hadn't. Not a great horsewoman in the first place, the lack of stirrups and reins reduced her to little more than a passenger clinging desperately to her mount's mane while squeezing with her legs for all she was worth. It took so much effort, she couldn't even enjoy the princess bouncing and jiggling a little bit ahead of her.

At least they'd met no one on the road and seen no sign of lizardman activity. Riding out in the open like this, just the three of them, felt like asking for trouble. Not that they had much in the way of options. No one would come looking for the missing dragon ship for at least another day and no way would Her Majesty wait that long.

So Mia clung on for dear life and watched every direction with her enhanced senses.

"You need to relax." Joran rode up beside her, seeming more at ease than he had any right to be. "You're holding your body too rigid. Feel the horse's movement and try to match it. Your flow should be making it easier for the mare, not harder."

She understood at once what he meant and eased the tension in her shoulders and thighs. The words didn't help so much as what she felt through their link. Mia still didn't know what to make of it. In all her days, first in the orphanage, then on the streets, and finally in the Tiber City Watch, she'd never had anyone willing to care for her the way Joran did.

Oh, she'd had a few men say they did, but they only wanted sex. When she showed no interest in that, they quickly moved on. But Joran's care and concern felt different, disconnected from desire. More pure.

Mia didn't know how to put the feeling into words, only that she knew beyond a shadow of a doubt that he'd always have her best interests at heart, even if they conflicted with his own desires. He'd already shown that once when he agreed to serve the princess rather than let Mia be separated from the woman she loved.

Why she loved Alexandra was another matter altogether. Certainly the princess was beautiful, but a commoner like Mia, and Alexandra, a member of the imperial family, had no real hope of a relationship. At least not an official one. And over the last day it had become painfully clear that the object of her affection regarded her as nothing more than a tool to be used or discarded depending on her needs at the moment. Perhaps that had always been true and Mia simply wouldn't see reality.

Just thinking that caused her physical pain, but she refused to keep living in denial. Joran had shown how much he'd give up for her, so Mia had a duty to at least face the truth. In the end, maybe getting reassigned as his bodyguard would be the best thing to happen to her. It would put some distance between her and Alexandra and maybe give her a chance to really figure out what she felt and why.

Above all that though, the idea of keeping Joran safe filled her with the warmest, most pleasant feeling she'd ever experienced.

"That's much better," Joran said, bringing her back to reality.

Mia realized when he said it that she was now copying exactly the way he rode his own mount. "Thanks. Is horseback riding something they teach all the nobility?"

"No. Father insisted my brothers and I learn to ride both in the saddle and bareback. He said that when you were in the field, you never knew what might be required. Frankly, I prefer a carriage, but I can manage like this if necessary."

Mia hadn't met many noblemen, but the few she had met were nothing like Joran. Usually the princess ordered her to stay behind when she went to the capital. Those dismissals had hurt and now she couldn't help wondering if Alexandra just didn't want her to cause any embarrassment.

She stewed on her situation as they rode and Joran kept silent, as if he knew she needed time to think. Would she be able to tell what Joran needed? Perhaps, if she thought about something other than her own problems.

That idea stung as well, but she had to admit the truth. She'd thought about little beyond her own wants and needs since meeting Alexandra and joining the Iron Guard. Maybe the time had come for that to change.

CHAPTER 7

J oran had never visited a provincial capital and if he judged them all by Cularo, he had no desire to visit any others. They'd made good time on their ride south and the city wall appeared a few hours before dark. The little visible beyond the wall made him despair of finding true civilization. The tallest building, and the only one made of stone, had to be the governor's compound. That would also be where the military camped when not out hunting the local rebels.

They reined in outside the gates. A unit of ten soldiers dressed in crimson and gold tabards over heavy leather armor guarded the entrance. Each of the soldiers carried a spear and had a shortsword belted at his waist. They looked Alexandra up and down with considerably less than respectful gazes. To be fair, she looked nothing like a princess at the moment and had a figure plenty worth examining.

"Mind your manners!" Mia barked.

The soldiers shifted their gazes, with considerable reluctance, to Mia. As soon as they saw her, or more likely her uniform, they snapped to proper attention.

"Apologies, ma'am," one of them said. Joran hadn't paid enough attention to the various units and their symbols to recognize the fellow's rank. "How can we be of assistance to the Iron Guard?"

"You can open that gate so I can get these nobles safely to the governor's compound. We've already been attacked twice by lizardmen on the ride south. The sooner we have a wall between us and them, the happier I'll be."

"You heard her!" the spokesman bellowed. "Open the gate. On the double!"

The soldiers scrambled to obey and soon they were inside the wall. Joran blew out a breath and some of the tension went out of him. They should be safe here.

A dirt road barely wide enough for two wagons to pass led straight to the compound. Alexandra dismounted and Joran and Mia quickly followed suit. Joran's thighs and ass swore at him, but a minute or two of walking worked the kinks out. A few people were out and about, but none of them appeared at ease. Everyone he saw had the look of provincials, probably the poor and the desperate hoping for a new life on the frontier. If their furtive glances and hurried strides were any indication, they weren't liking what they found.

He glanced at the nearest building, a two-story wooden model in standard imperial design. The bottom floor appeared to be a general store and the top no doubt served as a home for the owner. One thing about the empire, whether north, south, east, or west, you always knew when you entered one of their towns. The only thing that changed about the architecture was that the material and decorations grew finer over time.

After a moment of reckoning he figured the trading post

was three streets to his right. Much as he wanted to get that matter sorted out, family business would have to wait until he had Alexandra's permission to withdraw. One didn't simply walk away from a member of the imperial family in the middle of the street.

"Where are all the natives?" Joran asked. "Surely at least a few want to trade peacefully with us."

"You'd think so, but so far we haven't encountered any." Mia's hand seldom wandered far from the hilt of her sword.

Alexandra glanced back at them. "Not long now. I can't wait to get some clean clothes. We'll need to get you fitted for a proper advisor's robe. And a platinum amulet with the Iron Guard symbol as well. That will make it easy for you to come and go. Mia, you'll take up your new position as Joran's body-guard immediately. Once we get changed, I'll meet with the generals. Their excuses for not bringing the local populace under control should be amusing at least. I'll give you tomorrow to take care of that family matter you mentioned."

Joran bowed his head. "Yes, Majesty."

Given the decidedly modest size of the town, the walk took only ten minutes. The governor's compound had its own wall, this one made of stone though only about twenty feet tall. The portcullis stood open and a unit of soldiers patrolled the area. Ten of them had the standard crimson and gold tabards but a smaller group of six wore crimson and silver.

One of the second group spotted them approaching. His eyes widened. "Majesty!"

Everyone immediately took a knee.

"That will be enough of that," Alexandra said. "I need someone to alert the generals of my arrival and tell them to gather in the meeting hall in one hour. These horses need tending and tomorrow someone will have to return them to the next inn to the north. Mia, you know the way to my chambers. Alert the servants that I'll be there shortly."

Mia bowed and jogged off.

For his part Joran felt like the odd man out so he held his peace. For the time being he'd follow the princess's lead and hope for the best. Not that he had any other choice.

"We expected you to arrive by dragon ship, Majesty," the Iron Guardsman said.

"As did I, but the natives brought it down. No one else survived and if not for Lord Den Cade, I wouldn't have either. Only The One God's grace allowed my safe arrival. Now we make the scaly savages pay for insulting the empire."

The soldiers clapped fists to hearts. Alexandra returned the salute and set out through the gate. Joran stayed a step behind, careful to maintain the proper protocol. He never imagined all those lessons his mother taught him would come in handy, but it looked like they would today. To the left of the castle, three dragon ships sat on their flat-bottomed hulls, the balloons that carried them aloft inflated just enough to keep them from collapsing on top of the ship.

"Walk beside me, Joran," Alexandra said. "If you're to serve as my advisor, you need to get comfortable being at my side."

Joran seriously doubted he'd ever be comfortable by her side, but he took a quick stride and moved to walk at her right shoulder. "What happens now?"

"Now I get proper clothes, you get your robe and amulet, and finally we go see how badly those fools have screwed up this campaign. These primitives should have been dealt with months ago. Instead, they've tied up three legions plus my Iron Legion. Father is not pleased and when he's in a bad mood, even I get nervous."

"I hope I can be of some use, Majesty."

"Oh, you're entirely too clever not to be of some use. In fact, I have high hopes for you. And when we're alone, call me Alexandra. I get enough 'Your Majesty' this and 'Your Majesty' that from all the suck-ups here and in court."

They entered the castle proper and she led the way through an austere entry chamber, down a carpeted hall, and up a set of stairs. With each turn they passed soldiers dressed in crimson and gold. At the top of the stairs, she turned right, passed three closed doors, and finally strode through an open one.

Mia waited just inside along with six young women dressed in white tunics and sandals. Their dark hair and eyes marked them as imperials, but probably not nobles. The servants weren't half-ancient, but they weren't far short of being as beautiful.

Why couldn't Mia have fallen in love with one of them? He flicked a quick glance at his soulmate, but she didn't react. Instead, she stood at rigid attention, her gaze locked on the entrance as if she feared an imminent attack. Despite the pose, he sensed no actual fear in her.

"I need a full wardrobe change." Alexandra pointed at two of the servants. "You help Joran get cleaned up and find him an advisor's robe. We must have one around here somewhere."

Orders given, Alexandra swept through a door to the right, four of her servants on her heels. The remaining two girls looked at Joran and trembled faintly. No doubt they'd had bad experiences when told to help a nobleman get ready. And who would they complain to? He doubted Alexandra would care if he made use of her servants in pretty much any way he wanted.

Lucky for them, he had no desire to abuse anyone, much less a pair of powerless servants. "Why don't you two find that robe while I wash up. Is there a room I can use?"

The pair relaxed and one hurried over to a door on the left side of the entrance. "Through here, my lord. You will find water and a towel. If you need anything else, don't hesitate to ask. We'll bring you the robe as soon as we find it.

"Thank you, ladies. Just knock when you have the robe."

Joran went into a modest bedroom. Aside from the bed, he found a nightstand with a pitcher of water and bowl, a dresser with a silver mirror, a wardrobe, and a padded loveseat. Much as he would have loved to find out if the bed felt as comfortable as it looked, he lacked the time.

He washed up and opened his alchemy kit. The leftover water and towel were perfect for cleaning his used equipment. Once that was done, he secreted a couple of vials into pockets hidden in his tunic and trousers. Nothing lethal, but should a quick getaway be necessary, they would come in most handy.

Joran had barely finished his preparations when a soft knock sounded on the door. No doubt his robe had been located. Instead of the servants he found Mia standing outside with a crimson and silver robe. Though made of fine silk, putting it on felt more like donning a slave collar.

"I want you to know that I appreciate what you did for me." Mia draped the robe over his shoulders. "I'll try to be worthy of your sacrifice."

Joran forced himself to smile. "I'm just advising the princess, not getting my heart cut out. I'm sure it will work out fine."

The door opposite swung open and Alexandra strode out. Her hair had been combed smooth, her lips painted red and her eyes shaded deep blue. Joran looked closer. Was that Cade Cerulean? Her new robes were purple trimmed with silver and slit to reveal a length of toned, bronze leg.

Mia's reaction felt more mixed than he'd expected.

Certainly in any other setting a woman as stunning as Alexandra would have gotten his own pulse racing. With the princess, though, it was more likely to race with anxiety than desire.

"The new robes suit you." Alexandra pulled a platinum amulet out of her pocket and placed it over his head. It had the imperial eagle clutching a sword, the same as her gold one. "That marks you as my personal advisor. No one with a brain will give you any trouble while you wear it. The generals should be ready. Shall we see what they have to say for themselves?"

Without waiting for a reply, Alexandra strode out of the room. Mia and Joran shared a look before hurrying to catch up. Somehow, he suspected he'd be doing a lot of catching up in his new role. They made their way back downstairs and through rather plain halls before reaching an open pair of double doors. Inside five men waited around a rectangular table. The chair at the head remained unoccupied. The men stood for the few seconds it took Alexandra to take the seat at the table's head.

With no options for a seat, Joran stood behind Alexandra's chair and focused on the generals. Four of them wore crimson cloaks and gold-enameled breastplates. He shuddered to think how miserable that must be in the tropical heat. The final man dressed in all white save for a crimson circle, the symbol of The One God, on his breastplate.

A White Knight, terrific.

He should've expected to find some of the fanatics in Cularo. They always led the charge when the empire entered a new territory, eager to convert the heathens or, failing that, send them to whatever hell awaited nonbelievers.

The rest of the generals wore gold medallions marked

either with a number designating their legion or in the final man's case an eagle clutching a sword to indicate the Iron Legion. He must have been Alexandra's second.

"Well, gentlemen," Alexandra said after a moment of stony staring. "Explain to me why it is that the finest legions of the imperial army can't bring to heel a bunch of savages armed with stone-tipped spears."

The generals all started talking at once.

Alexandra raised a hand then pointed at the man with the five on his chest. "Caius, you first."

Caius cleared his throat and wiped the sweat from his florid face. Joran pitied the poor man having to walk around in this heat, much less having to do it squeezed into a breastplate. "Majesty, the problem isn't defeating the enemy in a fight. Anytime we get a chance to cross blades with them, it's a massacre in our favor. The problem is, the natives have realized they have no hope of defeating us in a straight-up fight, so they hit and run, hiding in the dense jungle where we can't reach them from the air and our forces are at a distinct disadvantage on the ground. We have yet to come up with a strategy to overcome their advantages."

Alexandra made no comment and turned to the church's representative. "And what do the White Knights have to say about this setback?"

The knight turned his dark gaze on Alexandra. He had hollow cheeks and a hawklike nose. His lean body gave the impression that his faith had burned away everything unnecessary.

"The legions lack the faith to push through the jungle's dangers to reach the enemy's hiding places. Perhaps a decimation would put some steel in their spines."

"So your plan is to kill off ten percent of our forces before they even see the enemy? That may be the stupidest suggestion I've ever heard." Alexandra slapped her palms on the table and stood. "Gentlemen, I want detailed reports along with your suggestions in my hands in twenty-four hours. Once I've read them all, I'll devise our new strategy."

So saying, Alexandra turned on her heel and stalked out. Joran and Mia fell in behind her, neither certain what, if anything, to say.

No one spoke to them on the short walk back to Alexandra's chambers. The serving girls were waiting and Alexandra said, "Wine."

Instead of retreating to her bedroom, the princess made her way to the sitting room where she promptly dropped into an overstuffed couch. She pointed at the empty chair across from her and Joran sat.

She put her feet up on the table between them and rubbed her forehead. "You see what I have to deal with? Zealots and men too stuck in their ways to try anything they hadn't been taught at the war college. The problem is, for all my complaints, Caius is right. Fighting in the jungle isn't the army's strong suit. What do you think?"

The servant's return with a tray laden with a bottle of wine and two glasses spared Joran from having to answer immediately. She poured and handed the first glass to Alexandra and the second to Joran before withdrawing to stand against the back wall.

Alexandra sipped and grimaced. "What I wouldn't give for truly cold wine."

Joran brightened. "There, at least, I can be of assistance. Excuse me."

He set his glass down, went to his room, and returned with a vial filled with ice-blue liquid. He shook it, removed the cork, and added the tiniest drop to Alexandra's glass then another to his own.

She eyed the glass, shrugged, and took a sip. Her eyes widened. "Amazing. What is that?"

"Essence of Winter, highly diluted of course." Joran took his own sip. "My mentor invented it to achieve the rank of grand master. I packed a vial, but with all the excitement forgot about it."

"I've never even heard of it. From now on, I'll bring a supply anytime I go on a southern campaign. Or better yet, you can just make us some." She set the now-empty glass down. "Now, no more delays. What are your thoughts?"

Joran shook his head. "In all honesty, Majesty, I haven't the least idea. I know nothing about the natives, the jungle, or even what resources the empire has on hand. My ignorance combined with a lack of experience in military matters render any advice I might offer useless."

She smiled. "Good. The first thing you need to realize is this: information is the most valuable commodity in war. Had you just made up something in the hope of currying favor, you would have dropped in my regard. Tomorrow you two will go and deal with your family business while I read reports. Then we'll see. Right now, I'm going to turn in early. You'll be using the spare room where you changed."

With that pronouncement, Alexandra stood and marched into her bedroom, closing the door behind her.

Joran blew out a breath. He'd won the first round, thank The One God. A serving girl came to collect the wine but he stopped her. "Leave it please, I'd like another glass. If you have cups, I'd be happy to share. Working in this heat must be difficult."

The servants looked at Alexandra's door then hurried away.

While they were gone, he added another drop of Essence of Winter to the bottle and poured a second glass. He took it to Mia. "I know you're thirsty. Here."

She drank deep and blew out a sigh. "Thank you."

Joran grinned. "It's a bribe. I'm going to need your help figuring out what to tell her."

"I fear you'll be disappointed. My skills lie in combat not tactics."

"I guess we'll figure it out together."

After pouring the last of the wine for the servants, Joran went to try out his new bed. He found it every bit as comfortable as he'd hoped. Pity his mind refused to let him sleep. How was he going to turn into a military genius between now and when the princess expected her answer?

Sleep arrived before a useful answer.

CHAPTER 8

After a tense but delicious breakfast with Alexandra, Joran left his advisor's robe behind and set out with Mia to the trading post. He kept his platinum amulet tucked under his tunic out of sight. Joran would have left it behind altogether, but figured he might need it to get back into the governor's compound.

He'd expected to find the streets busier in the morning, but much like when they arrived, they passed only a few individuals or small groups as they walked down the dirt streets. The town's businesses appeared open despite the lack of customers.

"Where is everyone?"

Mia shook her head. She still wore her Iron Guard uniform. In fact, she'd slept in it. He knew this since the servants had dragged a cot into his room for her. Joran didn't mind. In fact, having his soulmate close gave him a sort of unconscious feeling of comfort. He hoped Mia felt the same even though she hadn't said anything.

"It's been like this for a month," she said. "The lizardmen have been attacking supply wagons and it's making people nervous. Word must have reached some of the other cities since new arrivals have slowed to a trickle. Until the army settles things with the natives, I fear life won't get back to normal."

Joran turned down the street that led to the trading post. The unassuming little building had only a single story and a small sign out front that read Den Cade Trading. Since most of their business came from foragers willing to risk the jungle to collect wood and other exotic goods, the recent attacks would do nothing to improve business. Combined with the manager's skimming, well, the trading post's days might be numbered.

"What's the plan?" Mia asked.

"I'm going to talk to the manager, fire him, and promote his assistant. Those were Father's instructions anyway. Since I have no actual idea about the day-to-day operations of a trading post, much less the rest of the business, I see no reason to deviate from them."

"Do you want me to wait outside?"

"Of course not. We're soul bound, remember? Where I go, you go and vice versa, at least as much as my new position allows." Joran grinned. "I can't wait until you meet Mother. She'll be horrified that my soulmate is a commoner."

"It doesn't seem to bother you."

"Why would it? I much prefer the company of those outside the nobility. My best friend is an assistant librarian from the provinces. He's much more reasonable than any noble I've ever met, as are you."

Her pleasure at his compliment warmed Joran's heart. He meant it, too. Most of the nobility were horrid, grasping, obnoxious pigs. There were a few decent ones, but far too few for the good of the empire.

Joran pushed through the trading post door and a bell

tinkled. The building only had two rooms: the front where customers traded and the back storage room. Ten half-empty shelves lined the right side of the room and a bar ran along the back in front of the storeroom access door.

"Looks like business is worse than I thought," Joran said. "Hello?"

"What's the point of the bell if they plan to ignore it?" Mia asked.

She made a good point and he had no answer. Joran moved to the middle of the room. "Hello? Is anyone here?"

"Coming!" a voice called from the back room.

A disheveled, sweaty provincial with long blond hair and a nose that looked like it had been broken more than once emerged from the storeroom. His filthy white tunic stretched across a massive gut. Joran had seen less appealing individuals, but not in some time.

"What can I do for you?" the provincial asked.

"I need to speak with the manager." Joran pulled a rolled-up scroll out of one of his hidden pockets. "My name is Joran Den Cade and I have a message from my father."

The man's throat worked as he tried to swallow. "I told him not to do it. I said Master Den Cade would figure it out. Please, it wasn't my idea, I swear."

"Back up. I assume you're talking about the embezzlement?"

"Embezzlement? No, aren't you here about him trading with the locals? Master Darsus goes out twice a week and trades metal and other raw materials for rare herbs and botanicals. I think he then sells them on to his own contacts. That's why our profits are so low."

This was so much worse than simple theft. "You are going to make me a list of everything Darsus traded to the natives.

Lie to me or leave anything out and so help me you'll hang beside him. What is your name?"

"Gris, my lord. I swear on The One God's name I'll tell all." He made a circle over his heart.

"Good, get writing. I assume Darsus is out trading with them now?"

"That's right. He left an hour ago and likely won't be back before five bells tonight." Gris pulled paper, ink, and a quill out from under the bench and started writing.

Joran motioned Mia a little ways away.

"Sounds bad," she said.

"It certainly isn't good. As soon as this fool finishes up, we need to get back and talk to the princess. If Darsus has been trading the lizardmen steel, it might change everything about their fighting strength."

"It still wouldn't be imperial steel, only the government has access to that."

"I know, but the difference between knapped flint and sharp steel is huge. Though if they have steel, it's strange that the lizardmen we saw were still using stone spearheads." Joran shook his head. "No point guessing right now. The list Gris makes for us will reveal much."

It took only minutes for Gris to complete his notes. Joran took the paper and started reading. He frowned as soon as he saw steel ingots and only twenty pounds of them. That wouldn't make enough spearheads for a century of soldiers, much less an actual army.

He glanced at Mia. "Do the natives even have the knowledge or tools necessary to work steel? From what I saw, they looked like a stone-age society."

Mia shook her head. "None of our forces have reached one

of their villages. They might live in caves without even the concept of fire for all we know."

Joran turned back to the paper. So many blank spaces needed filling in. The empire had made a lot of assumptions about their enemies despite having no actual idea of their level of technology. His frown deepened as he read the rest of the list.

He shot a hard look at Gris, causing the man to flinch. "Most of this is alchemical precursors. Do the natives have knowledge of alchemy?"

"I don't know, my lord," Gris said. "Master Darsus never took me with him."

"Okay, last question before we leave for the governor's compound. To whom is Darsus selling the items he gets from the natives?"

Gris looked away. "Den March Trading."

Joran's jaw clenched. Naturally it would be their biggest rival. They probably arranged for Darsus to get this job in the first place. Whether they knew about him selling to the enemy, Joran had no idea, but he'd be certain to mention the possibility to Alexandra. A nice, messy imperial investigation would teach the pricks to mess with the Den Cade family.

Joran dragged Gris out from behind the counter and pushed him toward the door. Some time in a jail cell would teach him the error of not reporting his superior's poor behavior sooner.

As they retraced their steps back to the governor's compound, Mia said, "You're planning something. I can feel the gears turning in your head."

"Gris here has given me a lot to think about. Hopefully I can get a message out to the capital. I'm going to recommend that Father shut down the trading post until the security situation improves and he can find a reliable manager."

"Will he take your advice?"

Joran barked a laugh. "Jorik Den Cade takes no one's advice. Except, occasionally, my mother's and only then with regards to the nobility. That said, I still need to let him know about the situation on the ground. At least when he ignores my advice, he'll do so with all the facts."

"What about our other problems?" Mia asked. "Try as I might, I've come up with no possible solutions."

"I have a couple ideas, but nothing we should discuss on the streets. Plus, I'd really like to hear what Darsus has to say about the natives. He might have some insight that will come in handy."

As they approached the compound gate, Joran pulled his amulet out of his tunic. "Can you arrange a party to capture Darsus when he arrives or is that something we need the princess for?"

"I can do it," Mia said. "Your amulet gives you that authority as well. In fact, just being a noble might be enough to command them. But don't worry, I'll take care of it."

"What will happen to me?" Gris's voice trembled as he spoke.

"You didn't turn in Darsus, so that will be a mark against you, but you did tell me everything I wanted to know when confronted." Joran shrugged. "I'll recommend leniency, but it's not up to me to decide. If any more questions are asked, answer them fully and honestly. That's your best hope for survival."

"I will, my lord, thank you."

The guards opened the gates as they approached. Joran turned his prisoner over and Mia spoke with someone else about Darsus. The whole process took only a few minutes and then they were on their way back up to Alexandra's room. He assumed they'd find her there working, and if not that the servants would have an idea where to look.

The door was shut when they arrived. Barging in seemed like a poor idea, so he reached up to knock.

Before his fist could come down, the door opened and the Iron Legion commander appeared in the entrance. He stared at Joran with an angry sneer twisting his lips. The heat flushed his skin and sweat ran down his face.

"Enjoy your new position while you can," he said. "She'll likely be bored with you in a month."

Joran blinked at the venom in his voice. "Have I offended you in some way?"

"Only by your presence distracting Her Majesty and clouding her thinking. We need the Iron Princess focused on our current predicament not pining over some noble fool from the capital." He brushed Joran aside and stalked downstairs.

Mia's anger at the commander's words flashed through him and he sent thoughts of reassurance. He couldn't imagine Alexandra pining over anyone, much less him. Unless the heat hadn't caused the general's flushed skin.

"Were the princess and her subordinate lovers?" Joran asked.

"I don't believe so, but she often left me behind when she traveled, so anything's possible."

Joran stepped through the open door and found Alexandra reclining on the same couch where they spoke the evening before. She wore only a thin silk shift that clung to her in a most fetching way. Judging from the feelings flooding their link, Mia agreed.

The table held a stack of papers divided into two piles. She looked up with a scowl but her expression immediately smoothed when she saw him. "I didn't expect you two back so quickly. I trust all's well in the city?"

"No, things are not well." Joran told her everything he'd learned. "With any luck the guards will have Darsus in custody tonight. The lizardmen's interest in alchemical ingredients is disturbing, far more than them getting a few pounds of steel. I haven't fully analyzed the list, but it looked extensive. Who knows what trouble they might have brewed up. Assuming, of course, that they somehow learned alchemy."

"It seems impossible," Alexandra said. "Do you think that's how they brought down my dragon ship?"

"I've been thinking about that. I saw it when your ship exploded. It blew outward. That implies that the explosive was inside already. I'd need to study the wreckage to know for sure."

"How did a bunch of lizardmen get an explosive into my ship from the outside without anyone noticing?"

"I doubt that they could and that worries me even more."

Alexandra stood and paced around the room, her bare feet slapping against the smooth stone. At last she stopped and looked at him. "You understand what you're implying?"

He nodded. "That they might have had help, human help."

"If you're right, we need to know for sure. Take whatever soldiers you need from the Iron Legion. Mia can command them. Investigate the crash site and figure out what brought the ship down. If you're right and it was sabotage, that at least frees us up to use the dragon ships in our assault on the natives. If not, then we need to figure out how they got the explosive on board so we can guard against it." She waved a hand at the pile of papers. "From what I've read, we have no chance without the ships."

"With your permission, I'd like to wait until after Darsus is interrogated."

"No, this is too important. Write down any questions you have, but I need you two on your way as soon as possible. And do be careful. I'd hate to lose my new advisor so soon after finding him."

She didn't need to worry, careful was Joran's middle name.

———

Draq waited at the edge of the clearing where he met the human trader for their exchanges. He'd been listening to the man approach for ten minutes. He thrashed through the jungle making more noise than a half-starved hatchling. Draq's forked tongue darted out, tasting the human's sweat and fear. Despite doing business with them for months, Draq and his tribe still frightened the human.

Good, fear would keep the human's mouth shut. Fear and greed. Samaritan assured them that as long as they gave the human what he wanted, he would continue to trade with them. Draq shook his head, his scales rustling as they rubbed together. A member of the tribe would sooner cut off his own tail than betray his people to the enemy. Yet the humans spent as much time scheming against each other as they did their foes. It astonished Draq that they'd accomplished all they had.

"Can I kill the human this time?" Draq's second-in-command, Trina, asked. The female warrior had dark, almost black scales that matched her personality. She asked the same question every time they met the merchant and he always gave the same answer.

"Not this time. Samaritan says we still have uses for him."

Trina hissed. "You put too much faith in the humans. I've

seen Samaritan when he thinks no one is looking. The hate and anger twist his face into a demon mask. He's using us to fight the empire."

"Perhaps, but we are using his knowledge as well, so it's a fair trade. Without the information and allies he's provided, the tribe would have already fallen. You know this to be true."

"Yes, but I don't have to like it."

The human merchant staggered into the clearing, a heavy pack on his back. The stink of the chemicals he carried burned Draq's throat.

"Hello?" the human said, his voice trembling.

Draq stepped into the clearing. "I am here, human. You have the material?"

"You have the blossoms?"

As always, once the trading began, the man's fear receded as greed surged to the fore.

Draq crooked a clawed finger and Trina joined him with a woven basket in each hand. Purple blossoms filled the baskets to the top. The human's eyes widened at the sight. Why he valued the useless things remained a mystery to Draq. You couldn't eat them and they had no medicinal value. He'd asked Samaritan once and he simply shrugged and said that as long as they had something the merchant wanted, nothing else mattered.

"Wonderful." The human shrugged out of his pack and set it on the ground. "How do you find so many?"

"This is our home, human," Trina hissed. "We know all its secrets."

Draq placed a restraining hand on her shoulder. Her temper flared all too quickly.

"You are satisfied?" Draq asked.

"Oh, yes." The merchant grabbed the baskets and left his pack behind. "Same time in two weeks?"

"Of course. Safe travels." Draq waved and the human hurried back the way he'd come. When he'd moved out of earshot Draq turned to Trina. "Follow him."

Trina slipped into the jungle, silent as a breeze. Draq didn't particularly care if something ate the merchant, but he still had his uses and until that changed, he would make sure the human stayed safe.

Grabbing the pack, Draq turned toward camp. The warriors kept their distance from the villages. While he had little fear of the humans tracking them, when it came to protecting the mothers and young, best to take no chances.

An hour of hiking brought him to a clearing where a hundred of his followers lounged. A single tent sat in the center of the group. Draq's warriors had no use for temporary shelters. Their scales protected them from pretty much everything the jungle sent their way. Stone huts in the villages guarded the young and their eggs from predators, but other than that, they had no use for the trappings of civilization.

Their human temporary ally—and Draq harbored no illusions about Samaritan's loyalty to his people—had other needs. His warriors nodded as he made his way to the tent.

"Samaritan, I have the supplies."

The human emerged from his tent. He wore a filthy white cloak with the hood drawn up over his face. Battered armor dotted with rust glinted in the dim light and the hilt of a sword poked out by his left hip. Draq had once caught a glimpse of Samaritan's face without the hood shadowing it. He didn't know what the human had encountered to scar him so, but Draq dearly hoped never to meet one himself.

Samaritan took the bag and pawed through it, nodding to

himself. "Everything we need for another batch of weapons is here. I'll return to the lab and prepare them in the morning. I also need to check on the miners' progress."

"They must be getting close to the weapon," Draq said.

"I thought so as well, but as the days pass my confidence dims. Your people will not know peace until the imperial army is destroyed and for that we need the weapon." Samaritan pulled the bag shut. "Perhaps tomorrow will be the day. We can but hope."

The human turned to duck back into his tent. Draq shook his head at the man's odd ways. He'd gotten used to them in the six months Samaritan had aided them against the empire, but sometimes they still struck Draq as bizarre. And that was saying something for a human.

He hadn't even left his place by the tent entrance when Trina came sprinting into the clearing. She panted for breath and stood doubled over. How far had she run to be so exhausted?

"What happened?" Draq asked.

Samaritan emerged to join him, the bag left out of sight.

"The merchant was arrested at the gate of the human city."

"The imperials must have learned he was trading with you," Samaritan said. "The army should have at least one inquisitor with them. If so, he will quickly tell them all he knows. When he does, they will accelerate their efforts. We need to buy time if we're to locate the weapon before the empire finds your villages."

"What do you suggest?" Draq asked.

"Attack the city and destroy their dragon ships. The legions are hopeless in the jungle, but from the air they might get lucky."

"There are too many," Draq said. "You've told us that many times."

"Too many for a straight-up fight. But if you use the weapons I made for you and strike fast, you have a chance. You can always retreat at the first sign of organized resistance. It's a risk, I don't deny that, but I think it's one you need to take. These are your people, so the decision is yours. Whatever you choose, I need to get back to the lab." Samaritan got busy taking his tent down, seeming no longer willing to wait until morning.

Draq left the human to his preparations. He had a raid to plan.

CHAPTER 9

Marching down the road surrounded by soldiers dressed in armor and carrying tower shields and spears made Joran feel far safer than riding bareback with nothing but his thin robe to protect him. On the other hand, a day and a half of marching made his legs and back ache. He'd need to get more exercise if his new life was going to look like this, an hour a day clearly wasn't enough.

As they approached the site of the crash, his mind drifted back to the moment he saw the dragon ship explode. Whether due to his enhanced clarity or the trauma of the moment, every detail appeared clearly in Joran's mind. And with it came the memory of Clodius and his mother. He still hadn't found the boy's father. He'd certainly been busy enough, but that was no excuse.

Joran resolved that as soon as they got back and made their report, he'd find the man and tell him everything that happened. The poor fellow had to be frantic given the lateness of the carriage.

A faint hint of smoke reached him. Not far now. A quarter mile later they turned off the road and marched into the jungle. Twenty men needed a far wider path and soon spears were traded for swords and the front four started hacking. Lucky for them imperial steel cut wood and vines as easily as it did flesh.

After considerable grunting and cursing they reached what remained of the dragon ship. It looked much as Joran remembered. More of the balloon had fallen from the canopy and it looked like the lizardmen had claimed the bodies of their dead. The real trick would be figuring out exactly where the explosion happened given the amount of damage the ship had sustained.

"I want a perimeter set up around the ship," Mia said. "No one get sloppy. The enemy can sneak up on you far too easily in this environment."

The soldiers dispersed around the wreckage. Joran left them to their work and opened his kit. Assuming the explosion came from some sort of alchemical explosive, he'd need revealing powder to find it. Happily, he always carried a large supply. Never knew when there might be something interesting to study.

"Can I help?" Mia asked.

"Absolutely." Joran held out a pouch to her. "Sprinkle a little bit of this anywhere you see blackened wood on the hull. If anything glows, stop and let me know."

"That's it?"

"To begin with. We just need to know where to start the more detailed analysis. Also keep an eye out for tracks or signs that the natives dragged off anything heavy. The princess didn't give me a full cargo manifest, but if it looks like they made off with crates or anything else valuable, she'll want to know."

"Got it." Mia went left and Joran turned right.

He ignored the front of the ship. The explosion blew out the middle of the hull, so they needed to focus there. The first few spots he checked didn't react and from the smell he guessed they caught on fire after the initial explosion. So much had burned he had trouble telling one sort of fire from another.

Half an hour later Mia said, "Joran, I found something."

He scuffed the dirt to mark his place and hurried to join her. Mia stood beside a section of hull that glittered like the night sky. The planks had shattered and splintered leaving an awful mess. A few of the dark spots held a tinge of red. Some unfortunate crew member had been too close when the blast went off. Then again, maybe he'd been one of the lucky ones.

He bent closer to a particularly bright section of wood. Some residue definitely covered it. Maybe he could scrape off enough for a proper analysis. "This is great, thanks. I think you found the center of the blast."

Her smile warmed his heart. What she said next chilled the good feeling. "I haven't seen any bodies. There's usually a crew of twelve and Her Majesty never travels alone. A squad of Iron Guards at a minimum should have been aboard."

"The lizardmen must have taken them. I wager they'll have claimed any weapons as well. Weapons of imperial steel this time."

"Only a squad's worth, that can't be enough to change the tide of the war."

Joran took an empty vial from his pocket and drew a dagger. "They're already winning the war. Better weapons will make their raiders more effective which will curtail trade even more. No trade renders the city pointless as a business hub. Cularo will be reduced to a simple garrison town which does little to nothing to increase the empire's wealth."

When he'd scraped enough residue to fill half the vial Joran straightened. "This should be sufficient. Hopefully it doesn't confirm my worst fear."

"Which is?"

"That someone planted a time-delayed alchemical bomb in the dragon ship's supplies. The compounds used to make one are specific. I'll find out for sure in an hour at most."

"I'm going to scout around the crash site, see if I can figure out which way they took the bodies. Maybe I'll get a hint about where they live." Mia returned the pouch he'd given her and hurried away around the debris.

Joran hoped she found something, but wasn't optimistic. The lizardmen moved through the jungle like a fish through water, leaving no signs. Or worse they might lay a false trail to lead anyone following into a trap.

He shook his head. Best to worry about something within his control. A few minutes' work saw his portable burner lit and the restoration fluid heating. Once it bubbled, he added the residue he'd collected and let them meld together. Now he had to apply patience. Rushing the melding would be a disaster.

Time lost all meaning as he focused on the process. If you forgot about the jungle, heat, and potentially murderous locals, he might have been back in his lab at the college. The liquid slowly darkened to the correct color for testing.

When it got close, he pulled a collection of testing strips out of his kit. His hand was halfway to the vial when Mia's fear hit him like a sledgehammer.

He looked up to see her sprinting his way.

Only now did he notice the ground shaking.

"What's going on?"

The answer sent trees crashing to the earth as it stomped into the clearing. The beast stood at least thirty yards tall on legs as big around as tree trunks. A serpentine neck ended in a head that seemed far too small for the rest of it. Thick, greenish-yellow scales covered it like armor. Worst of all, one of the natives stood on its head, a staff adorned with all manner of fetishes held in a two-handed grip and pointed at them.

Looked like they'd walked into a trap after all.

———

Mia walked around the far side of the wreck looking for some sign of where the lizardmen had taken her fallen comrades. Even though the other members of the Iron Guard held her in low regard as a commoner, she knew if it came to a fight, they'd stand shoulder to shoulder with her to protect the princess.

She frowned at that idea. Protecting Her Majesty now fell to others. Mia had been dismissed, her duty now to keep Joran safe.

The frown vanished when she thought about her soulmate. Even now his intense focus came through their link. Since deciding to accept the position of advisor, he'd done everything possible to fulfill that obligation. Their link laid bare all his emotions as he went through his daily dealings with the princess and her servants. Jealousy no longer stabbed at her when she felt him looking at Alexandra. Not that Mia didn't still desire her, more that she'd come to accept that she meant nothing to the woman she'd dedicated the last three years to loving and protecting.

A hard thing to swallow for sure, but the truth often hurt.

She paused to examine some scratch marks on the ground. A moment of study confirmed they came from some kind of bird looking for food. Damned savages. They had to be here somewhere and when the legion found them, they'd be dealt with once and for all.

A vibration ran through the ground, shaking the trees and sending dry fronds falling. Mia had served in Stello Province for six months and never felt a tremor. Another one followed a moment later. Too close together for an earthquake.

She peered through the trees and squinted. With her vision enhanced by the soul bond she spotted something huge moving through the trees. She had no idea what the thing was, but she had no desire to fight it with her small force.

"Form up for withdraw!"

Joran gave no sign of having heard her, his entire focus on his work.

Mia sprinted toward him.

"What's going on?" he asked.

Trees crashed into the clearing and behind them came a giant monster with a lizardman standing on its flat head. She'd never seen or heard of anything like this creature. If the natives had such monsters under their control, why hadn't they turned them against the legions before now?

She shook the pointless question away. They could figure it out once they were safe.

"We're leaving." Mia snatched up his kit.

Joran collected the items he'd been working on and followed her to the edge of the clearing where the soldiers waited.

The lizardman loosed a horrible screech and the monster turned toward them.

"I don't think we can outrun it," Joran said. "It looks like the lizardman is a shaman and he's controlling the creature through magic. Fascinating. I've never seen magic at work. I'd heard stories of demon-worshipping warlocks among our enemies, but seeing it in person is another matter."

"Be impressed later. Run now."

Mia took his hand and they crashed through the jungle surrounded by their guards. They were all good men, but against that monster, Mia held little hope for victory.

"How do we kill it?" one of the Iron Legionnaires asked.

"We don't," Joran said. Mia glanced at him, but he didn't appear to have lost his mind and he seemed calmer than he should have through their link. "The monster isn't the problem, the shaman is. We eliminate him and the beast will have no direction."

"We have no bows," Mia pointed out. "And he's too high for spears."

Trees crashed behind them as the monster entered the jungle in pursuit. With its strides, their lead wouldn't last long.

"Are any of you good at climbing?" Joran asked.

She understood at once what he intended and she also knew none of the men in their heavy armor could do what he wanted.

"It has to be me." Fear for her safety washed over her. "Yes, it's risky, but with my enhanced abilities, I have the best chance of success."

"In that case, we'll do it together. Since we don't know the limit of our link yet, anything else is too uncertain."

Now she feared for his safety. The idea that Joran might be harmed filled her with dread. Unfortunately, she also knew that he was right.

"Turn left and stay just in front of that thing," Mia said. "We'll run ahead and set the trap."

The soldiers grunted an acknowledgement and she put on a burst of speed, dragging Joran along behind her.

"A hundred feet should be enough," he said.

At their mad sprint half a minute should do it. As soon as she spotted a tree sturdy enough for what they had planned she stopped and thrust the alchemy kit into Joran's hands. "Get out of sight. This will be for nothing if you get stepped on."

"Good luck." He trotted off and hid behind a tree.

Despite his calm tone she sensed his worry. Mia didn't blame him; she felt plenty worried herself. But with the vibrations getting closer by the second she had no time to dwell on them.

Wrapping her arms around the smooth tree trunk, she started climbing. Soon she reached some heavy branches and the task grew easier. When she reached a height about equal to where she figured the lizardman would be, she went up another five feet. A downward strike with all her weight behind it would have the most power.

She'd only get one chance at this and Mia planned to make it count.

Drawing her sword, she slipped around the trunk out of sight.

A minute later the guardsmen ran past.

Mia needed all her concentration to keep from falling off her branch as the beast got closer. A weird, musty funk filled the air as it closed in on her position.

Its head passed her and she leapt.

The lizardman swung his staff and to her utter shock her sword didn't cut through. Her weight and momentum did part of the job, driving the lizardman back and sending them both tumbling down the monster's spine before they slid off its back to the ground.

Mia twisted, landing on her feet, and sprinted toward the lizardman.

Without its controller, the giant beast staggered around like a drunk after a long night at the tavern. She dodged feet big enough to pulp her with a single stomp.

When she finally got clear of the creature, she found the lizardman on his feet. His yellow eyes glowed with an inner light and he pointed the staff at her.

Vines shot out, wrapping around her arms and legs, binding her in place. Even with her enhanced strength struggling did no good.

Her opponent raised his staff and took a step toward her.

The lizardman screamed and thrashed, spinning away from her to reveal its partially melted back and neck.

The vines loosened just enough for her to jerk free.

A single swing took the lizardman's head off.

Mia spotted Joran a few feet away and hastened to put some distance between herself and the now-docile beast.

"You okay?" he asked, relief flooding both his voice and their link.

"Yes, thanks to you. What did you hit him with?"

"Acid. I always keep a few vials handy for moments like this. I figured you'd take him with your first hit. What happened?"

"His staff resisted my sword. What kind of wood can stand up to imperial steel?"

"I haven't the slightest idea." Joran walked over and collected the fallen staff. "But it would be prudent to find out lest we run into more enemies armed with them."

"What say we figure it out later? Let's find the guards and

get to the inn. You can finish your experiments then we can return to Cularo in the morning."

"Works for me." Joran shouldered his kit and they set out.

Between discovering the lizardman's staff and his ability to control that monster, Mia had a bad feeling matters were about to get worse for the legions.

CHAPTER 10

Alexandra reclined on her couch, sipped chilled wine, and smiled. She should have brought an alchemist on as her advisor years ago, if only for the pleasure of a cold drink. How such a delightful invention had escaped her notice boggled her mind.

Behind her two of the servants waved large fans to try and relieve the miserable heat. She wore only a thin shift and even that felt like too much. The sooner she got out of this wretched province the happier she'd be. Unfortunately, the locals were making her task considerably more difficult than it should have been.

She'd spent the last day doing nothing save reading her generals' reports. Most of it amounted to little more than excuses for their failures. Despite that, she'd found a few suggestions in common. First, no one thought for a moment that trudging through the jungle in search of the enemy would bring good results, except Antius, the White Knights' representative. That arrogant fool would have her men march into the jungle and keep going until they dropped, ever confident that

The One God would see them through if only they had strong enough faith. She had little use for the zealot, but politics demanded that she not simply banish him from her sight. More's the pity.

A tiny voice in the back of her mind muttered that the empire would be better off if they forgot about the south and focused their expansion either north or west. The southern environment left the soldiers far too weak compared to the lizardmen.

It wouldn't do of course. One of the empire's founding principles stated that The One God's faith had to be spread to every corner of the planet.

Second, if the ground wouldn't work, that left the air and the dragon ships.

Alexandra agreed wholeheartedly with this and as soon as Joran returned with proof of how her ship had been brought down, she meant to launch an aerial campaign that would burn the natives out once and for all.

She chuckled softly. The look on General Ventor's face when Joran walked into the meeting behind her still brought a smile. Her second-in-command had ambitions beyond the military and he seemed to think Alexandra held the key to his future. That she found the man personally repugnant didn't seem to discourage him in the least.

Now he saw Joran as a rival. She shook her head at the stupidity on display. Her father would decide her future when he saw fit and Ventor would certainly have no say about it. Neither would Alexandra for that matter. She just hoped whoever Father chose for her didn't turn out to be too disgusting.

An explosion jarred her out of her random thoughts.

"What the hell was that?" She jumped off the couch and

hurried to the nearest window. It faced the eastern wall and aside from a few tiny figures running north, all appeared calm.

The thought had barely crossed her mind when a ball of blueish flames sent two of the soldiers flying off the battlements.

Alexandra marched into her bedroom and tossed her sweat-soaked shift aside. A suit of special lightweight armor custom-made for her from layers of alchemically treated cloth hung from a mannequin. First, she donned an under-tunic then the armor went over her head. It covered her from neck to thighs but remained flexible enough to allow full freedom of movement. Next came leggings and sandals followed by her sword.

While her talents lay mostly in strategy, Alexandra had studied the sword since age six, so anyone thinking her an easy target would quickly learn the error of their ways.

Someone pounded on the door and she strode across to answer it before the servants had a chance. Ventor stood outside in full armor, a look of disbelief creasing his arrogant face.

"What's the situation?"

"The city is under attack," Ventor said. "A force of natives has breached the north gate using alchemical explosives. All settlers and guards are retreating to the governor's compound."

Alexandra hoped she'd schooled her expression better than her subordinate, but she understood his disbelief. Despite Joran's report that the corrupt merchant Darsus had sold precursor chemicals to the natives, she'd never really believed they possessed the knowledge to make use of them.

It seemed they'd badly underestimated their opponents.

"How large a force are we dealing with?"

"Unknown at this time." Ventor's face twisted. "There's a lot of unknowns. I've got the Fifth and Sixth fully deployed to defend the compound with support from our military alchemists. The Iron Legion is protecting this building and the Seventh is in reserve."

"Good. Let's get to the roof and see what we're dealing with."

She brushed past him and found three squads of Iron Guards waiting in the hall. They formed up around her as she marched toward the roof access. First Squad pulled down a ladder and hurried onto the roof to make sure it was safe. The moment they signaled, Alexandra climbed up.

The castle's flat top made a perfect observation post. Pity she saw nothing that pleased her. In the city, buildings burned, dark smoke filling the air. Distant screams indicated that not all of the civilians had made it to safety.

The dark, scaled forms of the lizardmen darted through the streets. They maintained no formations, which made counting them difficult.

"Majesty, there." Ventor pointed at a quartet of lizardmen riding some sort of two-legged lizards about six feet tall with short, thick tails.

"They have cavalry?" she asked. "I read nothing about that in any of the reports."

"This is the first I've seen them, Majesty. Likely the enemy held them in reserve for this moment."

"Makes you wonder, doesn't it?"

"Majesty?"

"What else do you suppose they've held in reserve? Just how badly has the army underestimated this enemy? I thought we were dealing with stone-age savages limited to hurling sticks and rocks. Their only advantage was supposed to be knowledge of the local terrain." She rounded on him and waved a hand at the chaos. "Look at this!"

Ventor flinched away from her and Alexandra forced her mind to calm. Much as she wanted to rage, the responsibility lay with her for trusting her subordinates with pacifying this province on their own. Had she realized what they faced, she would have returned south sooner.

"Never mind. We'll hold the compound until all the civilians are safe. Then we sweep them out of the city. My best guess is we're dealing with a few hundred lizardmen, agreed?"

"Yes, Majesty."

"With our alchemists backing them up, the Fifth and Sixth should have little trouble dealing with such a small force while the remaining legions protect the compound. Get signal men up here, trumpet and flag, we can direct the counterattack from this position."

Two Iron Guardsmen ran to carry out her order. She took comfort in knowing that they, at least, wouldn't disappoint her.

It took most of an hour, but Caius finally signaled from the gate that the last of the civilians had entered. Alexandra had spent that time trying to figure out what the lizardmen had planned beyond lighting every building in the city on fire. If they had a grand strategy, she had yet to deduce it. Maybe they hoped destroying most of Cularo would convince the empire to leave.

If so, they didn't know the empire. Retreating would be a sign of weakness and her father would never allow such a thing. If he had to, the emperor would order every spare legion south with orders to burn the jungle to the ground no matter how long it took. That would be a total waste of resources not to mention bring shame on Alexandra.

No, they needed to deal with this and the sooner the better.

"Order the Fifth and Sixth to advance."

Trumpets sounded and the flagman nearest her waved an intricate pattern. As soon as he finished, the gates opened and the legions marched out. Nearly eight thousand men to deal with at most a few hundred savages. It felt like swatting a fly with a war hammer. But at this point, as long as the fly ended up dead, she didn't care how big a hammer it took.

The Fifth turned north and the Sixth south. They spread their lines as wide as the streets allowed and marched, shields raised and swords drawn. Clearing the streets would be easy, but Alexandra had spotted natives ducking into houses and climbing on roofs. The latter proved to be a poor idea and several natives fell, pierced by multiple arrows.

Alexandra felt her focus narrowing and made a conscious effort to survey the entire city. And it was well that she did. She turned west just in time to watch a thick vine streak out, grab a soldier off the governor's compound wall and yank him to the ground.

A moment later more vines crawled up the wall followed in short order by a dozen lizardmen. Their plan finally made sense. With everyone focused on the battle outside, this group planned to destroy the dragon ships. Without those, the army had no hope of victory, at least not anytime soon.

"Sound the alarm! Enemy inside the compound!"

One of the trumpeters blew a fanfare and soldiers boiled out of the castle.

A wall of stone exploded up, blocking them from reaching the dragon ships.

Seventh Legion soldiers patrolling the grounds rushed to intercept the saboteurs. Both sides hurled explosive vials.

Soldiers flew one way and natives the other. The survivors slammed into each other, hacking and slashing.

The imperials had numbers, but the natives had magic. A stone fist flew out of the ground and sent a trio of legionnaires flying.

Alexandra spotted the shaman a moment later standing just inside the wall. The yellow-scaled native held a staff over its head and capered around in some sort of dance.

"Priority target," Alexandra said. "Northwest corner near the wall."

More trumpets were followed by flag signals. Soldiers ran around the battlements, avoiding the wall of earth and readying their bows.

Arrows were loosed only to clatter against a hastily raised earthen dome.

That at least cut off the shaman's magic, allowing her soldiers to cut down the last of the saboteurs.

"The enemy is retreating," Ventor said.

"I knew it! They were a distraction to allow an attack on the dragon ships. Thank The One God we stopped them in time. Signal Caius. I want the city swept and those fires doused. Let's go see if we can dig out that shaman."

"I'll do it," Ventor said. "You should stay here where it's safe."

Alexandra shot him a hard look. "The day I need you to protect me, I'll retire from the army."

The Iron Guards formed up around her and they descended to the ground floor, emerging from the castle just in time to watch the wall of earth collapse. She frowned. Why would the shaman give them free access to the western quadrant now?

A queasy feeling hit Alexandra and she picked up the pace.

When they reached the earthen dome, that had collapsed as well. Forty nervous soldiers surrounded the pile of dirt. They stared at it and held their spears leveled like they expected the earth to try and kill them.

Not an unrealistic fear given the shaman's magic. Unfortunately, Alexandra had a different fear.

"Someone get shovels," she said.

Having an order to carry out seemed to calm them and a group trotted off to find some digging equipment. While they waited for the men to return, a youthful message runner came sprinting up to the group. "Majesty, General Caius reports that all the enemy have fled the city and disappeared into the jungle."

"Has he swept the city for stragglers or is he just guessing?" Alexandra asked.

"The sweep is underway as we speak, Majesty."

"Good. Tell Caius that I'll expect a detailed report when he's finished."

The messenger hurried away just as the soldiers returned with half a dozen shovels.

"Don't stand there staring at me," Alexandra said. "Get to work."

Half an hour of digging revealed a tunnel that looked like it ran under the wall. So the shaman survived to trouble them another day. A pity, but at least the dragon ships were unharmed.

"Apologies, Majesty," the unit commander said. "If we'd been a little faster…"

"No apology needed. When magic is involved, we can only do our best. See to the wounded then return to your patrol. I don't intend to be taken off guard again."

He saluted and barked orders to his men.

Alexandra turned to one of the Iron Guards. "I want this tunnel sealed. Have one of the alchemists see to it."

He saluted and hurried off to find one of the military alchemists. Until it was done, she wouldn't feel secure in the castle. Though now that she better understood the native shaman's abilities, she doubted she'd feel safe even after they'd sealed the tunnel.

———

Draq urged his runner out of the human city and into the jungle. The huge, two-legged lizard obeyed with ill-concealed excitement. His mount hated the city as much as Draq did, though obviously for different reasons. Many of his raiders had fallen in battle and the group he'd sent to destroy the humans' flying ships had failed. Despite the dead humans and burned buildings, the mission had ended up an utter failure.

Beside him on a runner of her own, Trina hissed in pleasure. Blood dripped from her talons and she licked it off. For her, killing humans would never be a failure. He wished he had the luxury of such simple reasoning. Now they had to pull back, creating a false trail away from their settlements lest the humans find them.

But first he stopped and studied the jungle. They had to be close.

A moment later the ground erupted and Voxel emerged, staff leading. Bits of dirt clung to his yellow scales and he wiped them off. Draq relaxed a fraction. The loss of his warriors stung, but losing a shaman would be a disaster. The tribe only had two.

"Apologies, Chieftain. The humans reacted too quickly for

us to destroy their infernal flying machines. As you commanded, I fled when victory became impossible."

"No apology needed, Voxel. You did all you could." Draq held out a clawed hand and helped the shaman swing up behind him. The slender lizardman added almost no weight to the runner's burden.

When they'd put more distance between themselves and the city Trina guided her runner over beside his. "What do we do now?"

"We'll put a day between us and the city. Once that's done, you'll keep watch and ambush any humans stupid enough to follow. Voxel and I need to return to the Holy Ones and warn Samaritan. Our failure today will force him to speed up his plan, if that is even possible."

"My wards will slow the humans," Voxel said.

"Good. I just hope they slow them enough."

CHAPTER 11

Joran blew out a breath and sat up, his neck and back popping. They'd arrived at the inn, the same one where he'd cured Alexandra, a few hours before dark. Kora had greeted them with a jaundiced eye, but again offered rooms. The total lack of traffic meant she had no one else staying at her inn.

He went straight to work as soon as they got settled. Mia rested on one of the uncomfortable cots, her presence a bit of warm reassurance in the back of his mind. They'd only been soul bound for a week or so and he already found himself completely comfortable with her psychic presence. It felt like something he didn't realize was missing had returned.

She sat up. "All done?"

"With that portion of the analysis. Unfortunately, my worst fears were confirmed. The explosion came from a delayed-blast device and there's no way the natives made it."

"How can you be so sure?"

"Do you remember that list of chemicals? One of the items needed to make this particular substance was missing and as far as I know it can't be found in this part of the world. No, I fear someone planted the device in the princess's dragon ship before it took off. Even worse, I fear whoever set it is working with the lizardmen. How else explain so many of them searching the area when the ship went down?"

"Her Majesty won't be pleased to hear your report."

"Maybe, maybe not. Remember, she wants to use the dragon ships to attack the natives. If the explosion came from somewhere else, it'll indicate that it's safe for her to follow her plan. Now for the last test before I finally get some sleep. Ready?"

Mia stared at him for a moment. "I don't know anything about alchemy. How can I help?"

"Simple, you can swing your sword for me. I checked the shaman's staff and I can't detect any magic. I assume that whatever force allowed it to deflect your sword came from a spell. But the only way to say for sure is to test it again." Joran stood and held out the staff. "No need to make a full swing. Just try and slice a piece off the end."

She got up and drew her sword. Mia looked as nervous as he'd ever seen her and their link confirmed the feeling.

"What's wrong? You just fought a magic-using lizardman riding a giant monster, but I swear you're more tense now."

"I don't want to mess up your test."

He smiled. "You can't mess it up. Either the sword cuts or it doesn't. If it does, then we confirm that it's just ordinary wood. If it doesn't, then we confirm that there's a naturally occurring substance that imperial steel can't cut. Both useful things to know, but hardly earthshaking discoveries."

"Right." She relaxed a fraction and made an easy swing.

The sword sliced clean through the last four inches of the staff with such ease that he barely felt it tug in his hand.

"Yup, it was the magic. First thing in the morning we'd best head back. She'll want to hear what we discovered."

Mia dropped back onto her bunk and sighed. "Do you think we can win this war?"

Joran sat on his own bed and cocked his head. "Of course. Why, do you think we can't?"

"Not exactly, it's just something about this campaign feels weird." She turned her head a fraction to look at him with half-lidded dark eyes. "I have nothing to back that up, you understand. It's just a feeling, but I trust it."

She sounded like some of the veteran soldiers he knew rather than a woman in her early twenties.

"Well, I trust you, especially given my lack of experience when it comes to war. That said, I have studied imperial history and the empire has never retreated from any enemy. If we can't win, the army will likely be destroyed."

———

Joran smelled the smoke before he saw it—too much smoke for the evening cook fires. Two days of steady marching had brought them to the outskirts of Cularo. He hadn't gotten this much exercise maybe ever and Joran's whole body wanted nothing so much as to settle into a hot bath for a long soak. Sadly, he feared the smoke meant his bath would have to wait.

"Something's wrong," Mia said. "Smells like a battle, but the lizardmen wouldn't dare attack the city center, would they?"

Joran shook his head. "If they had a couple more monsters like the one we saw, the wall certainly wouldn't slow them down much. Still, taking on four legions, even with a few monsters on their side, would be asking for trouble."

They didn't have to wait long to confirm Mia's fears. The gates had been destroyed, blown to pieces by alchemical bombs. Joran recognized the scorch marks. Only a beginner got results like that. The marks certainly argued that the natives' knowledge of alchemy hadn't advanced very far. And thank The One God for that.

A hundred soldiers, half on the ground and half on the hastily reinforced battlements, defended the ruined entrance. They all looked grim, as if expecting a fight at any moment.

The centurion in command raised a hand to stop them. "Identify yourselves."

Mia took the lead. "We are the investigative unit dispatched by Her Majesty to determine what brought down her dragon ship. What happened here?"

The soldiers visibly relaxed, not that they should have been too worried given everyone save Joran wore an Iron Legion uniform.

"The natives attacked the city. They had alchemical weapons and some rode strange, two-legged beasts. Bastards burned half the city before retreating." The centurion looked around as if fearing who might hear. "We took a bad hit. The generals didn't have a clue about the lizardmen's capabilities. Word is, Her Majesty is not pleased."

Joran believed that. "If that's the case, we'd best not keep her waiting. With your permission, Centurion?"

"Right, in you get." He waved them through.

Up close the damage looked even worse. The buildings nearest the gate had taken the most damage and many were little more than blackened shells. Further in, the buildings were still black, but it looked like some of the interiors had survived. Eventually they passed small groups of people picking through what remained of their lives.

Joran debated swinging by the trading post, but with no one to run it, there seemed little point in worrying. Assuming the army ever got things under control, Father could send a team to rebuild.

"What a mess," Mia muttered. "I never imagined the natives would try something so bold. It feels desperate."

"Why would they be desperate?" Joran asked. "The army hasn't done more than modestly harass them for months. They were winning without risking something this large scale. Unless there's a lot more of them than we think, the lizardmen couldn't have imagined they had a chance of winning."

Mia shrugged as they approached the governor's compound.

A random thought popped into Joran's head. "Where is the governor anyway?"

"There isn't one yet," Mia said. "The emperor won't assign one until the province is under control. I heard Her Majesty discussing it with General Ventor."

"Wise decision."

Members of the Iron Legion guarded the entrance to the compound and quickly waved them through. Mia nodded to the officer in charge.

"Where can we find Her Majesty?" Joran asked.

"Either in her suite or meeting with the generals," he said. "She does little else since the attack."

Mia dismissed their guards and asked, "What do you think, the suite or the meeting room?"

"The suite. If she's not there now, she will be eventually. I don't know about you, but I need a drink and some decent food."

"Food would be good," Mia said.

Joran glanced at her out of the corner of his eye. When they first met, she would have insisted they find Alexandra at once no matter where she might be. Unless he missed his guess, a fair bit of her devotion had worn off. Why, he didn't know, but he wished it had happened before he agreed to serve as her advisor. Though given the state of things, if his service could be of use to the empire, he had an obligation as an imperial noble to do his utmost to help.

They made the now-familiar walk to Alexandra's suite and found the door closed. Joran knocked and a moment later one of the servants opened the door. The beautiful young woman offered him a bright smile. "Welcome back, my lord. Her Majesty is in a meeting with the generals."

"Thank you. I trust you and your fellows weren't harmed in the attack."

She looked away as if embarrassed that he'd ask. "No, the creatures never breached the keep. Please, come in. You must be weary from your journey."

They stepped inside and she closed the door. The other servants stood quietly in the back of the sitting room. Two of them held large fans. Alexandra's attempt to beat the heat he felt certain.

"Could we trouble you for some food and wine?" Joran asked.

"No trouble at all, my lord." She leaned closer and whispered. "Whatever you gave Her Majesty to make her drink cold has done wonders for her mood. We are all most grateful."

"I'm happy to hear it. When we get back to civilization, I'll have to make certain to prepare another batch."

She bowed and hurried toward the kitchen. Joran went to his room to wash up and Mia followed. He tossed his tunic on the bed and poured water into a bowl. While he washed his face she said, "They're servants. You can just tell them what you want and they'll do it."

"Is that how it works?" Joran turned and grinned. "Trust me when I say, politeness is cheap and will earn you more than gold when applied at the right time. All these girls get are orders. Most nobles view their servants about the same way they view their horses. But they're not, and if you give them a little kindness and respect, you'll get far more in return. Works the same with innkeepers or any other worker you might run into."

"You're the oddest noble I've ever met, not that I've met very many during my time with the princess."

He tossed a clean white tunic over his head. "I'm likely the only one you've met that was raised by both a noblewoman and a common man. Mother taught me how to act in a way that befits my station and Father taught me when to ignore all that and just be a decent person. I'll leave you alone to wash up."

Joran closed the door behind him and went to sit on the couch. The servants holding fans came over and started fanning him. He sighed. The breeze felt wonderful.

A few minutes later the other servant emerged from the kitchen with a plate of meat, fruit, cheese, and bread as well as a bottle of wine and glasses. Eight glasses, bless her optimism. He added a drop of Essence of Winter to the bottle and poured them all drinks. He handed them out, keeping one for himself and one for Mia who emerged from the bedroom looking much refreshed.

She licked her lips. "That looks delicious."

They set to eating and sure enough the food tasted every bit as good as he'd hoped.

Stomping footsteps sent the fan bearers back to their places while the kitchen girl collected glasses and hurried back to hide them. Joran shook his head at the display and popped the last piece of cheese into his mouth. He doubted Alexandra would care if the girls had a glass of wine.

He kept his opinions to himself and he and Mia stood as the door opened. Alexandra stormed in, her face red and probably not from the heat.

"Where have you two been?" she demanded.

"Completing the mission you gave us, Majesty," Joran said.

Alexandra blew out a breath, some of the anger going along with it. "And?"

"Do you want the good news or the bad news?" he asked.

"I need some good news."

"Okay, the natives didn't bring down your dragon ship. Someone snuck a time-delayed alchemical bomb onboard. I suspect they're working in concert with the lizardmen which would explain why we encountered so many in the area of the crash."

"So your good news is that we have a saboteur working in the logistical department that oversees loading our dragon ships? And that said person is working in concert with our enemies here?" She wiped sweat from her brow and flicked it away. "I hate to hear your bad news."

"We encountered a native shaman at the wreck. He was waiting in ambush with a giant monster. Mia defeated him so she can tell you about it better than I can."

Alexandra shifted her dark gaze to Mia who cleared her throat. "The creature stood about thirty yards tall and must have weighed several tons. The shaman controlled it with magic that also allowed him to make his staff so hard my sword failed to cut it. At one point he bound me with vines. Only Joran's timely intervention allowed me to escape and strike the fatal blow. Despite the threat we escaped with no casualties."

"So they have more than one sort of monster in their army." Alexandra tapped her chin in thought. "At least they have no air power. That means we can go ahead with the dragon ship attack. We have over a hundred gallons of alchemist's fire. Hopefully that will be enough to burn them out of their hiding places. Well done, both of you."

"Thank you, Alexandra," Joran said, remembering at the last moment her order to call her by her first name. "I should say that I don't think the giant beast is a part of their army. Rather I suspect the shaman used his magic to bind it to his service since as soon as we killed him, the beast wandered off, seeming uninterested in a fight."

"The smaller ones I saw them using as cavalry certainly seemed well trained for combat, though I suppose some demon magic might have compelled them as well. Regardless, I'm giving the order for an aerial raid tomorrow. You will accompany me of course. Your insights have proven quite useful."

Joran bowed but inside his stomach did somersaults. He had no interest in being thousands of feet in the air should the natives prove to have air combat units of their own.

CHAPTER 12

J oran clutched his seat in the dragon ship's bridge and tried to think about anything besides how high they were. Despite his best efforts, nothing else came to him. At least they were fully enclosed. Unlike a sailing ship, everything in the dragon ship was surrounded by hull. The front of the bridge as well as—he swallowed hard—a section of the floor sported alchemically treated glass that gave the crew a clear view of everything ahead of and below them.

Alexandra stood in the center of the bridge, hands clasped behind her back, staring out at the sprawling jungle. She seemed totally at ease despite getting blown up in one of these things barely a week ago. Maybe as a member of the imperial family she'd spent so much time aboard them that she no longer thought about it.

Lucky her.

The rest of the crew consisted of two officers that oversaw the ship's steering. They occasionally shouted orders through tubes down to the crew manning the sails, but that was about it. A third member of the crew, this one a woman in her thirties, sat at a bolted-down desk covered with maps and other instruments. The final crewman sat looking down through the glass panel in the floor. Joran had yet to figure out his job beyond lookout.

Mia gave his shoulder a squeeze. She sat beside him on the passengers' couch at the rear of the bridge. At first, she'd tried to stand with the other members of the Iron Guard, but they made it clear they no longer considered her part of the unit. She'd taken it better than he expected and their link made it clear she wasn't faking her reaction. His annoyance at their behavior hit him harder than her own emotions.

"If it makes you feel better," Mia said. "As far as I know, the crash the other day was the first time a dragon ship has gone down."

Joran patted her hand. "It doesn't make me feel a bit better, but thank you for trying. How far are we going out before she gets started?"

As if in answer to his question the navigator said, "We should be right at ten miles out, Majesty."

"Good. Prepare the dragon head's cannons."

An officer flipped open the lid covering one of the tubes that let him shout orders to the crew on the decks below and repeated her order.

A minute later an unintelligible reply came out of the pipe. "Cannons ready, Majesty," the officer said.

"Release the first volley." Alexandra walked over to the viewing port.

Even from his spot on the couch Joran could see a stream of liquid fire roaring down into the jungle. The torrent continued for ten seconds. Half a minute after that Alexandra stomped her foot, far too close to the glass pane for his liking.

"First volley complete," the man beside her said, his tone formal. "Minimal damage to the trees and foliage."

Joran frowned. Even allowing for the wood's wetness, that much alchemist's fire should have done more than minimal damage. Assuming they mixed it right, and if there was one thing military alchemists knew how to make it was liquid fire.

Alexandra rounded on Joran like he'd done something wrong. "Those idiots assured me they'd made this batch extra strong and yet we can barely scorch the trees."

Joran stood and wobbled. Mia put a hand on his back to steady him. "Thanks. Is it possible to drop something other than alchemist's fire from the ship?"

"Of course it is," Alexandra said. "We have ports that let us lower ropes for the infantry to attack. We can drop whatever you want from them. Why?"

"Because even the most incompetent military alchemist can make more effective alchemist's fire than that. Something's suppressing it. My guess is more of the shaman's magic. I want to release a cloud of revealing powder to see for sure."

"I hate magic. Runner!"

One of the Iron Guard separated himself from the rest and strode over. Joran dug a half-full pouch out of his kit and handed it to him.

"Tell them to sprinkle it out, not drop the whole pouch."

The runner saluted and hurried out of the bridge. Joran winced and inched his way over to the glass panel. Just looking at the trees so far below sent his stomach into his throat.

"Stop being such a baby." Alexandra stomped her foot down full force on the glass. Joran nearly fainted. "You could hit this thing with a war hammer and not crack it."

"Sure, assuming whoever blew up your transport didn't treat the glass with something to weaken it. I can think of at least three compounds that would do the trick and you'd never know until you fell to your death."

She frowned. "Well, this one is clearly fine, so relax. You're making me nervous."

Easier said than done, but Joran tried his best.

"Sally port's open," the communications officer said. "The powder is going out."

Mia moved to stand beside him and stared. "What are we looking for?"

"The same glow you saw when we were investigating the wreck." Joran pointed. "Right there. Did you see the sparks?"

"I did," Alexandra said. "What do they mean?"

"Only that some magic is active down there. I assume it's an anti-fire ward of some sort. I know so little about the natives' magic, I can't say for certain."

"How big is it?" she asked.

Joran shook his head. "I don't have enough powder to find out for sure. If we assume they have an ally in the empire—"

Alexandra grabbed his arm and dragged him toward the couch. Mia's protective instinct hit him, but she kept herself under control. Luckily for all of them. That it had even triggered against Alexandra shocked Joran. The soul bond must have been even more powerful than his research indicated.

"We will not speak of that here," she whispered. Louder she added, "Is there something we can do to destroy their cover that the magic won't affect?"

"Yes, but it will be expensive."

She waved a hand. "I don't care how much it costs. This stalemate needs to end. What do you need?"

"An industrial alchemy lab and some engineers capable of modifying your dragon ship."

"I know just the place. Captain, send a message to the other ships to return to Cularo. We'll be heading to Fort Adana at best speed."

The second officer bowed and shouted orders down his voice tube. Soon the dragon ship lurched and they were on their way. Joran hastened to sit down. How did Alexandra stand traveling like this? He would have happily traded the dragon ship for a coach, ruts be damned.

————

Days of hard riding brought Draq and Voxel within sight of the forbidden mountain. Samaritan and the Holy Ones directed the search for the weapon that would allow them to drive the empire out of their territory once and for all. Darker than the surrounding peaks and shorter as well, the mountain wouldn't draw a second look from an outlander, but Draq's tribe had long known that the place was special.

To this day Draq didn't know how Samaritan learned about it, but the knowledge was one of the reasons he'd chosen to trust the human's warning about the pending invasion. He'd been right about the empire's intentions and about pretty much everything else he'd told them since. Perhaps the human had served his people as a prophet and been cast out. That would explain his drive for revenge.

He shook his head and guided the runner around the base of the mountain to a narrow, concealed trail that led up to an entry cave. The nimble animal climbed the path with ease. Outside the dark opening they dismounted.

"I will wait here," Voxel said. "The spirits of this place make my scales crawl. Perhaps I can strengthen the wards."

"Whatever you can do would be welcome." Draq squeezed his shoulder and slipped into the darkness. He'd learned long ago that when a shaman spoke of the spirits, all someone like Draq had to do was nod and accept.

His sight shifted immediately into darkvision and the tunnel appeared in blurry shades of gray. The rough floor had been smoothed by many feet, making the walking easy. Lucky for Draq, he didn't have far to go. Samaritan's lab waited only fifty strides from the entrance.

He slipped down a side path and blinked his vision back to normal. Glowing jars lit the cavern that held Samaritan's lab with a warm, golden light. The man himself worked hunched over a stone table covered with items Draq had never seen before. One bubbled over a flame. Another sat under a glass tube collecting liquid that dripped out.

Samaritan must have sensed his presence. The human pulled up his hood and turned to face him. "You failed. Nothing else would have brought you here."

"Yes. We destroyed much of the city, but failed to reach the ships."

"Unfortunate, but not surprising given the numbers you faced. The gambit always held risk. Now the imperials will be even more keen for your destruction."

"Voxel says they attacked the wards today and were turned aside."

"Good. If they can't use fire, the military alchemists will be at a loss. The fools never had an inch of imagination. That should buy us time. I checked with the miners today. They're getting close to the shaft where the weapon waits. All the signs point to it."

"That is good news. Even if all the tribes were to rally, we would have no hope of defeating the humans in open combat. What should we do now?"

"I advise you to call all your warriors back to defend the

mountain should the empire discover it. Bring the women and children as well if you think it wise. Whatever happens, it will be decided here."

Draq nodded once. "I will consider your words."

Samaritan said nothing more as he turned back to his workbench. One thing Draq appreciated about the human, he never tried to force Draq to do anything. He advised and let the lizardmen make the final decision themselves. When he'd first shown up offering his knowledge of the empire, Draq had feared he meant to try and take over. But that fear, at least, hadn't come to pass.

Leaving Samaritan to his work, Draq moved deeper into the mountain. Soon he heard the sound of steel on stone. The tunnel split left and right. Left led to the dig. Draq went right. He wanted to get the advice of the Holy Ones. If they agreed with Samaritan, he would bring the tribe here for the final battle with the empire.

The crude temple to the spirits of earth and sky held little beyond a stone altar and in the back a pair of sleeping pallets. Two figures knelt before that altar, their white scales seeming to glow with an inner light. The Holy Ones turned to face him. Identical in every way, the twins were born from the same clutch, the only young to survive. Among the tribes, the birth of identical twins happened at most once a generation and no lizardman had ever been born with white scales.

The tribe knew at once that they'd been touched by the spirits. As the pair grew older, all the evidence confirmed their unique status. Somehow they heard and spoke to the spirits even without the training a shaman received. It seemed as though they had as much spirit in them as flesh and blood.

"How can we help you, Chieftain?" the right-hand twin asked. Their mother never named them. Everyone called them

Holy One and they were so closely connected that sometimes it felt like one soul occupied both bodies.

"I need your advice, Holy One. Samaritan suggests we draw all our forces, along with the mothers and young, back to protect the mountain in case the humans learn of it. What do the spirits say? Is this a wise course?"

"The mountain spirit says we will reach the weapon soon," the other Holy One said. "But an earth spirit's sense of time and a mortal's may not match. If it takes longer than we hope, having a way to at least delay the enemy will be necessary."

Draq nodded. "And the mothers and young?"

"We leave that to your judgement. They will make no difference in the final battle. Do whatever you think will best protect them should the worst happen." The Holy Ones turned back to the altar signaling the end of the conversation.

Draq bowed at their backs and turned to leave. It seemed the Holy Ones didn't intend to make the decision easy for him. He retraced his steps and continued down the second branch. This walk took longer and soon the clang of the miners' picks rang so loud they hurt his ears. When he finally reached the end of the tunnel, he found four burly lizardmen swinging the picks Samaritan made out of the metal the human merchant traded them. Four slightly smaller figures hurried to load rock chips into baskets.

Aside from being ten yards longer, the tunnel looked exactly as Draq remembered. Not wanting to interrupt their important work, he retreated without speaking.

As soon as Draq stepped out of the cave it felt like a weight lifted off his shoulders. Voxel sat cross-legged on the ground, an aura the color of palm leaves surrounding him. The shaman opened his eyes and stood, the glow fading as he did.

"You appear troubled, Chieftain," Voxel said. "Did the Holy Ones not provide the guidance you sought?"

"They provided some of it." Draq told him what Samaritan and the Holy Ones said. "What do you think, old friend?"

"If the imperials find us here, we don't want our young nearby. Better if we leave them in the villages scattered through the jungle. Some of the old and young warriors can remain behind to protect them. Even if we all fall, the tribe will survive."

"Will it?" Draq asked. "Do you think the humans will spare our families if they win the battle?"

Voxel shook his head. "I don't know, but I do know that if we are all gathered in one place, we make their work easier for them. It is your decision, Chieftain, and I will support you no matter what."

Draq bared his fangs in a humorless smile. One more person telling him to make up his own mind. Just what he didn't need.

CHAPTER 13

Joran read the final page of Darsus's interrogation report. Alexandra had been kind enough to bring him a copy and the reading did wonders to distract him from the fact that he was sitting several thousand feet above the ground in a ship with a proven history of occasional explosions. The crew did their work with quiet competence and that helped a little as well to set his mind at ease.

Alexandra had withdrawn to her cabin to nap and she took the Iron Guards with her. That suited both Joran and Mia fine.

"Anything interesting?" Mia asked.

"Beyond the fact that Darsus was a greedy shit? No. He knew next to nothing about the natives beyond where they met and how often. One thing did strike me. It seems the natives made contact with him when he went out to see what he could scrounge up near Cularo. They said they wanted peaceful trade and that not everyone hated the empire."

"That's good, right?" Mia sat beside him on the couch.

"It would have been good if they hadn't also told him not to mention that they were conducting business. Not that Darsus would have risked losing his exclusive access, but if the natives truly wanted peaceful trade, they would have spoken to someone official, not a merchant."

"Maybe the lizardmen feared they'd be killed on sight given the hostilities."

Joran folded up the little packet of papers. "Doubtful. The empire hadn't fully gone to war with the natives when Darsus first met them. Peace remained very much a possibility. All the natives had to do was make contact, promise not to attack any humans, and say some nice things about The One God. As long as they behaved, the empire wouldn't have bothered them."

Mia smiled. "I suspect peace would have required more effort than you make out."

"There would have been more details, but when you boil it down, that's what they had to do. No, I suspect they wanted those supplies to make weapons and Darsus sold to them without a second thought. The fool claimed that he saw no harm in it since 'the savages don't know how to do alchemy.'" Joran threw up his hands in disgust. "As if they'd ask specifically for those compounds without knowing why. Darsus saw gold dancing in his eyes and convinced himself that what he was doing was okay."

"What's Her Majesty going to do with him?"

"If he's lucky, a visit to the headsman. If he's not, she'll ship him back to Tiber and have Primus Lucius publicly execute him as a traitor. I have little sympathy for someone whose greed got the better of him, but I wouldn't wish Primus Lucius's tender mercy on anybody."

"Fort Adana on the horizon," one of the officers announced.

"Want to have a look?" Mia asked.

"Yes, just as soon as we're safely on the ground."

She laughed, drawing a smile from him. He found that their

link made their moods infectious. For better or worse. Should they ever both be in a bad mood at the same time, he shuddered to think what might happen.

The dragon ship slowly descended. Joran looked away from the viewing window. Seeing the jungle getting constantly closer made him think they were crashing even though he knew they weren't.

At last the ship went still and the captain said, "Landing complete."

Joran stood. The sooner he had solid ground under his feet, the happier he'd be. Three flights of steps brought him to the exit ramp. Alexandra and her guards waited at the bottom with another man about sixty in a crimson and gold uniform. He stood straight and tall despite his white hair. A pin on his vest that resembled a vial crossed with a sword identified him as a military alchemist.

Alexandra beckoned him over. "Joran, let me introduce Gallus Ruso, the senior alchemist at the fort. Gallus, this is Grand Master Joran Den Cade, my personal advisor. Anything he needs, you will provide. Understood?"

"Yes, Majesty." Gallus bowed. "If you'd like a tour of our lab, we can get started. I just finished a batch of alchemist's fire, so the lab is freshly cleaned and ready for the next project."

"Perfect, Master Ruso," Joran said. "I look forward to working with you. If you'll give me a moment to speak with Her Majesty?"

"Of course, my lord." Gallus bowed and moved out of eavesdropping range.

Even so, Joran kept his voice pitched low. "How many soldiers can you spare?"

Alexandra frowned. "We have a full century of drop troops. They can be redeployed if necessary. We're far enough from the front that a raid should be no issue. In fact, we're not even in Stello Province anymore."

Joran looked around. "I'm not worried about a raid. I'm worried about someone sneaking a bomb on board while they're doing the modifications. Or maybe adding something that will spoil the compound I'm synthesizing. One will set us back days and the other will kill us."

Alexandra glanced around then back to Joran. "We didn't even stop at this fort on the way south. It's one of the more isolated forts in our network. That's why I chose it."

Joran shrugged. "Maybe nothing will happen. That would suit me perfectly well, but if there is someone here with ill feelings toward the empire, do you think they'll pass up another chance to take a shot at you?"

Her eyes narrowed before a slow, evil smile spread across her face. "If there is such a person, maybe we should invite them to set a bomb. We'll guard the lab but leave the dragon ship open. Anyone tries to sneak aboard or do anything destructive, the guards will grab them and we can have a long discussion. Focus on your work. I'll handle security."

"As you wish, Majesty." Joran bowed and went to rejoin Gallus with Mia in tow. "Apologies for the delay. I had a small matter to verify with the princess. Please, lead on to the lab."

Now that he had a moment, Joran glanced around the fort. It had a huge open area where dragon ships landed and soldiers trained. A number of large buildings made of tan stone surrounded the open area. The largest had to be the hangar where the shipwrights repaired damaged dragon ships. Another, he assumed, served as a barracks. Dozens of soldiers patrolled the battlements armed with bows and shortswords.

Gallus led them to the smallest building. Two soldiers out front hastened to open the double doors for the old man.

While they strained to pull the massive wooden doors open Gallus said, "I've read about you. The youngest grand master in history. Quite an honor."

"Yes, sir," Joran said. "There were some people who didn't approve of someone my age receiving the title, but I completed all the necessary qualifications, so like it or not, I received the promotion."

Joran remembered those arguments with considerable bitterness. The older alchemists seemed to imagine that time counted for more than skill and hard work. Like the many eighteen-hour days he'd put in counted for nothing. The only thing he actually looked forward to about his new position as Alexandra's advisor was seeing the looks on those old men's faces when they found out.

The doors clunked open and Gallus stepped through. Joran had visited an industrial lab before, though he'd never worked in one. The alchemy equipment looked the same only sized for giants. Hoists along with block and tackle hung from the ceiling to help with moving the massive equipment.

"So what are we making?" Gallus asked.

"Essence of Autumn, about a hundred gallons of it." Joran pulled the list of chemicals he'd need out of his pocket. He'd already upped the amounts by a thousand for industrial output.

Gallus took the list and frowned. "I thought we were to prepare a weapon to slay the rebels."

"We are, in a roundabout way. The enemy shamans have created an anti-fire ward to protect the jungle. This uses an entirely different process to clear the canopy and reveal the ground. Once we can see their hiding places, the drop troops can deploy and deal with them directly."

Gallus's frown didn't waver. "Is this enough to do the job?

As it is, we'll need to use our entire supply of several chemicals."

"Don't worry. Once the base is finished, we can dilute it a hundred to one with no loss of effectiveness."

"You certainly seem well informed about this compound."

The sound of clomping boots drew their attention to the front of the lab. Fifty of the drop troops had arrived and formed a semicircle around the entrance. Spears and shields formed a wall through which no enemy might slip.

Joran turned back. "I'm the foremost expert in the use of Essence of Autumn. I'm also its inventor. Rest assured, it will do what we need."

He glanced back at the soldiers. Assuming no one interfered with the production.

———

It took half a day for Joran to reach a point where he felt confident enough to leave the military alchemists to oversee the bubbling vats filled with brown sludge. It pleased Mia to see him in his element even as the process of adding and mixing chemicals bored her nearly to tears. For the first hour she'd been hypervigilant for any threats, but as it grew increasingly clear that no one intended to mess with the processing, she relaxed a fraction.

The princess had taken Joran's concerns to heart even as it seemed to Mia that she considered the threat minimal. Hopefully her former master would prove correct and her soulmate wrong. They needed no more problems on this mission and the idea that enemies of the empire might have infiltrated such a remote fort worried her a great deal.

"I appreciate your patience," Joran said as he marched away

from Gallus and his subordinates. "All they need to do now is maintain the temperature for twenty-four hours. After that we move on to the next process. Did they get the dragon ship moved into the hangar?"

"Yeah, about an hour ago." They set out side by side toward the massive building. "It barely fit through the doors. What's the next process?"

"Filtering. That's the easiest one. There can be no sediment or it will plug the emitters. If that happens, we'll have a real mess on our hands." Joran ran a hand through his short hair and a shot of his unease ran through her. "I still haven't found Clodius's father. Surely someone has told him what happened by now."

Mia shook her head. "I don't know. With the chaos of the attack, I doubt the fate of one family is anyone's highest priority. Don't be too hard on yourself. I can feel your tension. If you push too hard you might have a breakdown."

He smiled. "Thanks. With your help I'm sure I'll be fine."

Mia cocked her head in confusion. "My help? All I've done is stand around and watch you work. I'm useless for this sort of thing."

"You're wrong. Knowing you're here watching for any danger allows me to focus and do my job. Without you, I'd be constantly looking over my shoulder."

They reached the hangar and a thin harried-looking man hurried over. He wore filthy coveralls and a belt loaded with tools. His dark hair appeared slicked back with axle grease or some other equally nasty substance.

"You're the advisor?" he asked.

Joran nodded. "You spoke to Her Majesty?"

"My whole damn crew is here waiting to do whatever it is

you want us to do. So what the hell do you want us to do exactly?"

"I want you to install mist emitters in place of the dragon cannons. They'll need the same wide funnel for receiving liquid at the top, but the emitters themselves need to be as fine as possible."

"You mean like a watering can?"

"Something like it, but with far smaller holes. I need to make a mist, not a drizzle."

Mia did her best to hide her amusement at the dirty man's consternation. "We have nothing like that in the warehouse. We'll have to modify something or maybe even make them from scratch. How many do you need?"

"Two should be plenty."

The engineer grinned. "That's doable and I love a challenge. Leave it to us, Advisor. We'll have a mockup for you by morning."

"Excellent." Joran clapped him on the shoulder. "I'd heard the imperial engineering corps stood second to none when it came to fabrication. I can't wait to see what you come up with."

"We aim to please."

Before he could leave Joran asked, "Did you hear where the princess went?"

"I believe I heard her say she planned to have dinner with the base commander in the castle." He hurried off before Joran hurled more questions his way.

"You have a wonderful way with people," Mia said.

"People always expect the worst when dealing with a nobleman. All the more so when that nobleman is close to the imperial family. If you show politeness and respect, you've already far exceeded their expectations. What say we hunt up some dinner then see if we can find Alexandra?"

"Great idea, I'm starving."

Mia stretched and yawned. When she opened her eyes she spotted a figure sneaking around the corner of the hangar toward the rear.

Her hand went to her sword.

"What is it?" Joran asked.

"I saw someone. They looked awfully furtive if they weren't up to something."

Joran slipped a vial out of a pocket. "Let's take a look. I know Alexandra said she'd made arrangements, but better safe than sorry."

Mia raced around the corner of the hangar, sword drawn.

She froze at once. The man she'd seen stood with his trousers unbuttoned, a stream spattering his sandaled feet as he stared at Mia's sword.

Joran threw back his head and laughed. "Beg your pardon, sir."

Mia's face burned as Joran led her off toward the castle. "I'm sorry. I felt certain he was up to something."

"Don't worry about it. We're all keyed up. Better you speak than miss something. Besides, I needed the laugh. The look on that guy's face will keep me chuckling for a month."

Mia offered a sheepish smile. "I think the kitchen is usually toward the rear of the castle. I smell stew from here."

They walked side by side, Mia setting a good pace. She wanted nothing so much as to put as much distance as possible between her and the site of her mistake.

CHAPTER 14

Food at the castle kitchen turned out to be everything Joran expected: thick, filling, and of no particular flavor. Still, eight hours of constant work combined with his angry stomach on the dragon ship did wonders to make the bowl of mediocre stew palatable. In fact, it might have been a fraction better than the slop they served at the roadside inns.

Twoscore soldiers filled half a dozen benches while another handful stood in line to collect their bowl of stew. None of them looked up as they shoveled the food in as fast as possible. Maybe that was the trick—get the task completed quickly. If Joran's mother saw him eating like the soldiers, he'd never hear the end of it.

Beside him Mia ate with a will, seeming delighted with the meal. As a member of the Iron Guard, he'd assumed she would've gotten better food than this on a fairly regular basis. Either Alexandra was less generous than even his low expectations, always a possibility where a noble was concerned, or

Mia was the least fussy eater he'd ever met. Given her background, the latter certainly seemed possible.

Joran sniffed and caught a hint of burnt almonds. At first he assumed the cook had ruined dessert, then he remembered they didn't serve dessert.

Holding his breath, he dug through his alchemy kit. If it wasn't dessert, only one thing smelled like burnt almonds: a powerful paralytic. As soon as the thought hit him his hands started to stiffen up.

Across the hall a soldier collapsed off his bench with a dull thud.

Like an arthritic ninety-year-old, Joran frantically tossed vials and agents aside until he found a bottle filled with white pills. His lungs burned as his stiffened fingers wrestled the top off.

At last he shook a pill into his hand and tossed it into his mouth. As soon as it hit his tongue, the pill melted and his hands started working again.

Turning to Mia, he found his soulmate rigid as a plank, her hands twisted into claws and her eyes stuck open. Joran shook out a second pill and forced her mouth open just enough to pop it into her mouth.

A few seconds later she shuddered and blinked. "What was that?"

"Poison. A powerful paralytic. I nearly didn't notice it in time. Can you move?"

She stood, still stiff but mobile. "Where did it come from?"

"I don't know." Joran looked around as if he'd see someone fanning the stuff into the dining hall. His eyes widened. "Where would the commander's chamber be in this place?"

"If the castle follows standard imperial layout, second floor, left-hand corner. Why?"

"Alexandra. If everyone in the castle is paralyzed, she's a sitting duck. Lead the way."

Mia ran and Joran struggled to keep up with her. He would have liked to wake a few more of the soldiers, but didn't dare take the time.

They rounded a corner and raced up a flight of steps. Joran wheezed, but somehow made it to the top. Mia didn't even slow as she sprinted left.

He caught up to her just in time to see her cut the hinges off a closed door. She kicked it in and charged through.

Steel clashed as Mia fought a figure in black armed with a sword identical to her own. Alexandra and a man wearing a crimson and gold uniform lay stiff and unmoving on the floor beside toppled chairs. Joran would be of no use in a fight, so he hurried over to Alexandra.

When the pill he forced into her mouth had dissolved, her eyes opened and she stared up at him.

"You're safe now, Majesty."

Hopefully that was the truth.

———

M ia didn't know what the poison Joran negated had done to her, but as her sword clanged against the man in black's it nearly popped out of her grip. Her arms felt like overcooked pasta and her feet seemed to weigh about ten pounds each.

She batted aside a thrust and countered in what seemed to her to be slow motion.

The assassin slipped away from the blow and reset himself.

Mia had no doubt that without her link to Joran, she'd have been dead by now. As matters stood, the fight was a draw. On the plus side, her strength grew by the second. Half a minute more and she'd have the advantage.

The assassin seemed to realize it too. He drew a dagger and hurled it.

Not at Mia, but past her.

She tried to knock it aside.

Too late.

The dagger tumbled by.

Pain filled her a moment later and she knew Joran had taken the blow. Rage unlike anything she'd ever experienced filled her, blasting away the lingering effects of the poison and pushing her to the very edge of her strength.

A hard blow sent the assassin's arm flying before her back cut nearly decapitated him.

Mia calmed a moment later and only then realized that she should have tried to take him prisoner. Unable to lament the death of the man that had hurt her soulmate, she flicked the blood from her sword, sheathed it, and hurried to check on Joran.

He sat cradling his forearm; the five-inch dagger had pierced it right between the bones. Alexandra sat beside him, her eyes wide and staring at the dagger. Her hands trembled, but that might have something to do with the poison.

"Are you okay?" Mia asked.

"That might be a stretch." Joran offered a smile he meant to be reassuring but that came across as more of a grimace. "Would you be so kind as to get my kit? I left it beside the table where we were eating."

"Sure, just a minute." She sprinted off.

After that burst of anger, she felt back to normal. In the dining hall she found all the soldiers lying on the floor stiff as boards, some staring at nothing and others with their eyes closed. Joran still had the anti-poison pills, so she had no way to help them and no time even if she did.

Not entirely certain exactly what he needed, she took a moment to gather up all the odds and ends he'd tossed aside while looking for the antidote. Kit in hand, she ran back upstairs.

Joran had regained his feet and now sat in one of the righted chairs. Alexandra stood behind him, her hands resting on his shoulders, all signs of trembling gone. The fort commander had begun to stir, his soft groans filling the quiet.

Mia set the kit on the table in front of him. "What else can I do?"

"Find a container of dark-red paste. It's marked with a horizontal dagger."

She remembered that one. He'd tossed it out during his search. The little round container sat right on top and she opened it, confirming the paste inside. "What now?"

"Now the unpleasant part." Joran scooped up enough paste to cover the end of his index and middle fingers. "Pull the dagger out."

He grit his teeth and she yanked. The instant the dagger cleared the wound, he smeared paste on both sides. Mia watched as the wound sealed up and healed over until only a thin line remained.

Joran flexed his fingers and nodded. "Troll blood paste, wonderful stuff. Thank you, Mia. Majesty, are you okay?"

In all the excitement Mia only now realized that the princess hadn't spoken a word since the poison wore off. Assuming her jaw had unthawed, it must be the shock of nearly getting killed that kept her silent.

"I'm fine," Alexandra said. "Thanks to you two. I owe you both my life twice over now. When he threw that dagger, I saw it coming for me and my body refused to move. If you hadn't put your arm in the way…"

"It was my honor to take a blade for you," Joran said. "But Mia's the real hero. If she hadn't defeated that assassin, we'd likely all be dead."

They both looked at her and Mia squirmed. "Just doing my duty. Should I give antidote pills to the other soldiers?"

Joran shook his head. "I don't have that many and the poison isn't lethal in any case. The effects will wear off in an hour or so. Until then, perhaps we should have a look at our would-be killer."

There was a clunk as the commander tried to get up, drawing their attention. Mia blew out a breath of relief. She didn't like having everyone's attention on her, not even when it was just Joran and Alexandra.

"Help that idiot into a chair," Alexandra said. "How did an assassin slip into his command?"

"Doubtless the same way one slipped into a supply depot," Joran said.

Mia gently lifted the fort commander into the remaining chair. Joran stood and the three of them walked over to the dead man.

A solid kick from Alexandra flipped him over on his back. His mask covered the lower half of his face, but judging from his dark eyes and hair, the would-be killer was an imperial.

"Why would an imperial betray the empire?" Mia asked the obvious question.

"Excellent question," Alexandra said. "The One God knows that if the empire falls, none of us will be treated warmly by the provincials, much less the people of nations we haven't visited yet."

Joran bent then stopped halfway down as he clutched his newly healed forearm.

"What do you need?" Mia asked.

"I wanted to check his body, see if there's anything that might give us a clue. Though the wound is closed, I fear the damage isn't fully healed. Could I trouble you?"

Mia knelt and patted the dead man down. Another throwing dagger clattered on the floor followed by a bronze amulet. "That's it."

"The marking on the amulet," Joran said. "What is it?"

Mia handed it to him. Alexandra moved in for a closer look until their cheeks nearly touched.

"Looks like The One God's circle with a slash through it," Alexandra said. "Something like this would get you sent to the inquisitors. Who'd be dumb enough to carry it on them?"

"Someone not expecting to survive his mission," Joran said. "Someone that wanted it found on his body so everyone would know who killed the Iron Princess."

CHAPTER 15

Joran looked around the alchemists' supply room. Scores of chemicals in a variety of vials filled row upon row of shelves. His kit had gotten dangerously empty and he hoped to stock up while he had a chance. Unfortunately, the military alchemists didn't keep an especially wide supply of items on hand. They had the basics of course, as well as anything you might ever want to make things burn or explode. Healing items were also well represented.

He shrugged and slipped another vial into his bag. He needed to make some modifications, but that should be enough to see him through until they got home. Assuming Alexandra actually let him return home. Her gratitude at being saved seemed genuine, but it also seemed to make her even more determined to keep him and Mia at her side.

Speaking of his soulmate, he turned to see her still standing outside the entrance, hand on her sword as if she feared another attack. He admired her determination, but suspected that if another assassin lurked somewhere in the fort, they would have attacked together to make sure the job got done.

But then again you never knew and having her between him and trouble made Joran feel safer.

He thought of one more thing he wanted when the sound of faint footsteps reached him.

"Someone's coming," Mia said.

He hastened to collect the final item and hurried to join her out in the hall. When he arrived, he found a young man of perhaps eighteen years dressed in a crimson and gold uniform bowing to Mia.

"Everything okay?" Joran asked.

"Yes, my lord," the soldier said. "Her Majesty sent me to bring you to the morgue. Everyone has recovered and she and Commander Cybatus are waiting for you to examine the body."

Joran had no idea why they'd need him and Mia present for that, but he shrugged. If she wanted them there, then they'd go. "Lead on."

They followed their guide through the castle. The bare stone walls seemed especially grim after what happened. Every soldier they passed paused to touch fist to heart. Word of the attack must have spread. No surprise there. After an entire castle's worth of soldiers got paralyzed, you had to offer some sort of explanation. Though if they heard the whole, unvarnished truth, Joran would have been surprised.

The morgue turned out to be in the castle basement. Not very handy, but it would keep the bodies a little cooler. They found Alexandra and Commander Cybatus, now upright and seeming little worse for wear, standing on either side of a closed door.

Alexandra brightened immediately when they arrived. "Joran. I figured you'd want to be here when we looked closer at the body. Being a healer, you might notice something we miss."

"Isn't the fort healer overseeing the examination?" he asked.

"No," Cybatus said. "We, that is Her Majesty, deemed it prudent to keep the number of people aware of the assassin's identity and mission to a minimum."

"Prudent, though I haven't performed an autopsy since my student days. Shall we?"

Joran led the way in while Mia remained by the door to make sure no one accidentally entered while they worked. They didn't even need to discuss it, she just knew what to do, probably plucked the idea right out of his head. If he didn't trust her completely, that thought would have troubled him no end.

The morgue had four stone tables, only one of which had an occupant at the moment. The assassin lay on the nearest slab, his severed arm set at his side.

"Determining the cause of death won't be an issue." Joran drew his dagger and sliced the black mask off. "Do you recognize him?"

"Yes," Cybatus said. "Bartius, a military alchemist subcommander. He's been with us for a decade. What could have driven him to this?"

Joran hadn't wanted to believe an alchemist would betray the empire. Out of all its citizens, no one benefited more than alchemists from the empire's success. To betray it was to cut your own throat.

"We'll need everything you have on the man," Alexandra said. "Family, friends, past postings, all of it. Someone got to him and we need to find out if they got to anyone else."

"Of course, Majesty. Perhaps speaking with the other

alchemists would be wise. They may have heard him say something."

"I'm considering sending the inquisitors to investigate the entire fort," Alexandra said. "Make sure we have no other enemies in our midst."

Cybatus's gulp reached Joran from his position beside the body. A perfectly natural reaction when someone mentioned the Inquisition. If there existed a single group in the empire that no one wanted to deal with, that was the one.

Joran had only met a member once, when he sat for his interview to enter college. That humorless woman had asked him questions for most of an hour, many of them having nothing to do with his training or field of study. She seemed especially eager to ask him about his faith. Not a particularly comfortable line of inquiry for someone whose faith was more pragmatic than devout. He'd gotten through it with little more than an upset stomach and considered himself lucky.

"Wouldn't involving the church suggest that the army couldn't police itself?" Joran asked. "Surely you have some sort of investigative unit to handle this sort of thing."

"Of course we do," Alexandra said with a thoughtful look. "My concern is we have no idea how deeply the rot has penetrated. They might be fanatics, but in this situation, that makes me more inclined to trust the Inquisition. None of them would ever involve themselves with a group that denigrates the church."

Joran turned away from the body to face the others. "Do you wish my advice, Majesty?"

She managed a faint smile. "That is why I made you my advisor."

"Then I advise that you form a task force. Pick your best investigators then interview them under the effects of a truth potion. Once you've convinced yourself of their loyalty, send them here. Whatever needs to be done, give them the authority to do it. Then send them to the next fort and the next and the next until they've rooted out anyone disloyal to the empire. Keep the church out of it. The less they know about the army's weaknesses, the better."

"Are you certain you're a scholar and not a courtier?" Alexandra asked.

"I may dislike politics, but my mother made sure all her boys knew how to scheme and counter-scheme. And on a personal note, the idea of the church gaining any more power in the empire sits poorly with me. Far too many of the priests are already more arrogant than the worst of the nobility. Giving them any authority over the army is like throwing bloody meat into shark-filled waters."

"Very well. Once we deal with the rebels here, putting the team together will be your next task back in the capital. Any other alchemist might be compromised, as our dead assassin proves."

Joran kept his expression and tone neutral as he said, "As you wish, Majesty."

Inside he shouted at the universe. He was never going to get back to his lab.

———

A few quiet conversations with Gallus and the remaining alchemists convinced Joran that they knew nothing about Bartius's plans and further that they harbored no ill will toward the empire. He might have been wrong of course. Without access to a detect-deception potion he had no way to say for certain. Perhaps they were highly skilled liars, but he deemed the odds of that low. Most alchemists didn't have a politics-obsessed mother teaching them how to deceive like it was a professional qualification.

A full day of work saw the Essence of Autumn finished and loaded into the dragon ship's hold. The engineers had worked like mad to get the emitters attached shortly afterward. He had to respect their dedication.

Once the last man left, Joran and Mia entered the hangar. They had two hours until sunset and Alexandra had declared that they'd leave in the morning. That suited Joran fine as he wanted to give everything a thorough going-over. Damned if he'd end up blown out of the sky due to his own negligence.

"What are we looking for?" Mia asked.

"Anything out of place. I'm hoping if anyone has done anything, your enhanced senses will detect it." Joran pulled a pouch out of his pocket. "I've got revealing powder as well. Between the two of us, we should be able to check everything."

"Do you really think there's another traitor?"

"I don't know. I didn't really think there'd be a first one. I only suggested it out of an abundance of caution. Now my paranoia's even worse. I'm almost looking forward to getting in the air and away from anyone that wants to kill us."

They stopped in front of the emitters. The dispersal mesh stretched over the funnels looked fine. He sprinkled a little revealing powder and found nothing.

"The seams look okay," Mia said. "And I can't see anything inside."

Joran led the way around the ship. Every few steps he tossed a pinch of powder, checking for anything to spark and finding nothing. Mia remained silent as she followed, humoring him, Joran assumed. And that was fine. No one ever died from an excess of caution.

Once they finished with the outside they slipped into the hold, nodding at the Iron Guardsmen on duty. Alexandra had ordered her chosen people to watch over the ship which pleased him a great deal. If she'd considered him overly cautious before, nearly dying had done wonders to bring her around to his way of thinking.

A quick check of the barrels revealed no leaks and no loose seals. Essence of Autumn didn't spoil from contact with the air, but it did make an awful mess if you got it on your clothes.

Half an hour later they'd searched the entire ship and found nothing out of the ordinary. Satisfied that he'd done everything possible, Joran stretched and yawned. Seeing no particular reason to return to the castle, they descended to the second level and went to the tiny cabin they shared a door down from Alexandra's.

"You do remember," Mia said as they settled into their hammocks. "That we're about to fly into a war zone. Safety will be in short supply when we get back to Stello Province."

Joran chuckled. "I suspect safety will be in short supply wherever I end up as long as it's near the princess."

———

Joran jerked awake when the ship lurched. He took a moment to orient himself. Right, in a dragon ship on our way to a war zone. Basically the exact opposite of anything he ever imagined himself doing.

"Morning."

He turned and smiled at Mia. The only thing he didn't regret about his current situation was finding his soulmate. She had already dressed in her crimson and gray uniform and belted on her sword. A covered tray sat on the tiny table between their hammocks. With any luck breakfast hid under there.

"Morning. Are we taking off already?"

"The ground crew is just pulling us out of the hangar. Her Majesty boarded a few minutes ago. She had that look that said she was anxious to get back into the fight. Considering how she keeps almost getting killed lately, you'd think she'd be ready for a break."

"I know I am." Joran rolled out of his hammock. "But I fear none of us will be getting a break until the rebels are dealt with and even then we'll still have to put her investigation team together. Then maybe I can take you to meet my parents. Father will love you. Mother I'm less sure about. Is that breakfast?"

Mia stared at him, seeming not to have heard his final question.

"Hey? You still with me?"

She shook her head as if to clear it. "Sorry. You said you wanted to introduce me to your parents. That's a first for me. No man I've ever met wanted me to meet his family. No woman for that matter either. Though to be fair, I've never been very good with relationships. Just look at my obsession with the princess. It took meeting my soulmate to show me what real love is. How pathetic is that?"

Joran put his arm around her shoulders. "I'm glad I could do that for you. And no, it's not pathetic at all. Before I met you, the only thing I really cared about was finding the next compound in the lab. Now, if I had to choose between you and my work, I'd pick you every time. So, breakfast?"

Her glum expression brightened and she lifted the tray's lid. Underneath he found two bowls of now-cool oatmeal, toast, honey, and an apple for each of them. Not the greatest breakfast in the history of meals, but he hadn't eaten much since just before the assassin the night before last. Had that only been the night before last? It felt like longer.

He ate with enthusiasm and soon enough the food was gone.

"Delicious and thank you for bringing it."

The ship lurched again and the queasy weightless feeling settled over him. Looked like they'd taken off.

"I suppose she'll be on the bridge waiting for us," Joran said.

"No doubt. Are you ready for your second flight?"

"Not especially."

She helped him shrug on his advisor's robe and they made the climb up to the bridge. The Iron Guardsmen at the entrance nodded to them and one pulled the door open. They seemed to have a bit more respect this morning. Maybe Joran and Mia doing their jobs for them gave them a better appreciation for the pair.

Joran put the thought out of his mind and stepped onto the bridge. As he expected, Alexandra stood in her usual spot near the window in the floor. The same four crewmen occupied the same stations. The familiarity actually calmed him a fraction and nearly made him forget his trembling legs.

"Finally," Alexandra said. "I thought you two would never get up. I sent a messenger bird ahead so the other dragon ships will be airborne to meet us when we arrive. We're going to take another run at them and see if your new stuff works any better than alchemist's fire. So tell me exactly what it does."

"It does exactly what the name implies. If you hit a tree with it, the leaves will change color and fall to the ground. If you put a drop on a newly sprouted plant, it will quickly grow until it's ready to harvest."

"Interesting. How did you ever think up such a substance?" Alexandra asked.

"My mentor created the Essence of Winter you enjoyed so much in your wine. Two hundred years ago another alchemist invented Essence of Summer. Inspired by them, I decided to give autumn a try. It took me over a year of failures before I figured it out. My presentation won me the title of grand master."

"You must sell a ton of it to the army," Mia said.

Joran cleared his throat. "No. The army never showed any interest. They always prefer fire."

"What do you do with it?" Alexandra asked.

"Mostly Father sells it to nobles that want an autumn wedding in the middle of summer. A heavily diluted dose will turn the leaves and leave them at peak color for several days. He never said how much he charges, but I suspect it's a lot."

Alexandra threw her head back and laughed. After she wiped the tears away she said, "I need to speak to Father about raising the nobles' taxes. If they have enough to waste on something so stupid, they can afford to pay more. On a more serious note, we don't have days for the leaves to fall."

"I know. I left the mixture fairly pure. The leaves should turn and fall within thirty seconds."

"Should?" Alexandra gave him a look.

Joran shook his head. "It's an estimate. I've never used this particular formulation and I didn't have time to do a proper test. I based the dilution on what I'd done in the past, but until you try it in the field, all I can guarantee is that the leaves will turn and they will fall."

She muttered something unkind then shrugged. "I guess we'll all find out in a couple days."

CHAPTER 16

They reached the skies above Stello Province without blowing up, which pleased Joran immensely. What pleased him a great deal less was standing in the hold of the dragon ship, wind from the open emitter hatches blowing his hair around, and nothing but a far-too-slender rope around his waist between him and an accidental fall.

Doing his best not to think about that, he focused on the four burly men wrestling barrels filled with Essence of Autumn into position. The new emitters were in place and the wide-mouthed funnels ready. They needed only an order from above to start spraying.

Joran darted a glance out the open hatch. Nothing but jungle in every direction. He had no idea what Alexandra sought, but he wished she'd hurry up so he could get the hell out of the hold. She probably enjoyed the idea of him trembling down here. Plenty of nobles were sadists at heart, just like the inquisitors.

His silent cursing ended when the captain's distorted voice said, "Deploy when ready."

All four men looked at him.

"Just pour it in slowly. The emitters will take far longer to drain than you're used to with the dragon's head cannons."

They wrestled the first barrel into place, yanked the cork, and tipped it up. A small glob hit the deck, staining it orange. No way would they be getting that out. Thank The One God the wind blew in their favor today. A heavy breeze in their faces would have really messed things up.

He peeked again and saw an orange cloud filling the air below them. It looked almost like fog as it settled over a large swath of jungle. As soon as it hit the canopy, Joran started counting. At ten the huge leaves began to turn from green to orange. When he hit thirty-five, the orange and yellow leaves started to fall.

Revealed for the first time, the jungle floor appeared largely free from undergrowth. Probably because no sunlight reached through the canopy.

"First barrel deployed, my lord," one of the roughnecks said. "Do we release the second?"

Joran had no orders either way. "Let's wait a moment and see what the first batch reveals."

What it revealed turned out to be about a square mile of nothing. The second barrel misted out and he repeated the count. Happily, the numbers matched. Excellent. He'd have to make a note in his workbook for this formulation. Given the information he had for the other variations, he should now be able to calculate timelines for everything in between.

On the downside, the next section of jungle turned out to be as empty as the first.

Wait. He peered closer. That looked like a trail. From this high he couldn't be sure, but it appeared to run from northwest to southeast. He needed to tell Alexandra.

He took a step toward the speaking tube but his rope stopped him at once. No way was he taking it off.

"Send a message to the captain. It looks like a trail directly below us."

One of the roughnecks repeated the information.

A few seconds later the ship lurched and they were soon traveling southeast. When the trail vanished again beneath the canopy the captain said, "Deploy the next barrel."

They seemed to have things under control now. Joran backed away from the hatch until he stood beside the stairs leading to the second floor. He untied the safety rope and hurried upstairs.

Mia waited for him at the top. "I thought my heart might burst from your fear. Are you okay?"

"I'm better now that I have an entire floor between me and a long fall. I spotted a trail. Let's get up to the bridge and see if it leads anywhere."

"How can you tell it's the natives and not some beast?"

"I can't, but it's the only thing I saw that even hinted at civilization. Following it has to be better than just flying around and spraying at random. At least I hope so."

They reached the bridge and found Alexandra looking intently out the glass pane on the floor. She looked up when she heard them and her smile lit up the room. "Your compound is working brilliantly. The military alchemists told me it was a waste of time, but I knew better."

Joran grimaced at the idea of the military alchemists running him down behind his back. While he didn't especially want his new job, damned if he'd have his professional ability questioned.

"I appreciate your confidence, Majesty. And since they seem to have no trouble talking behind my back, do you know why there are so few grand masters in the army? Lack of imagination. Most of them still use the same formula for alchemist's fire that their predecessors did centuries ago. If they had an original idea it would split their head faster than lightning would a pumpkin."

Alexandra's laugh ended when the captain said, "Majesty, we have signs of habitations below."

She scrambled to the front of the bridge. "At last. Prepare to deploy drop troops. Tell them to let at least a few of the natives flee should they be so inclined. Hopefully the survivors will lead us to some of the other villages. Signal the other ships with the same order."

"Yes, Majesty." The captain relayed her orders through the speaking tube and the dragon ship began to descend.

Curiosity overwhelming fear, Joran moved to stand beside Alexandra by the window. Mia joined him a moment later. The lizardman village had been revealed in all its dubious glory. Twenty stone huts sat clustered in a clearing shaded by trees that grew at unnatural angles. No doubt due to more of their magic.

Green-scaled figures scrambled around as three hundred legionnaires descended via ropes. A few natives hurled stone-tipped spears that clattered harmlessly off the soldiers' armor.

"Is it me or do there seem to be few warriors among the group?" Joran asked.

"Most of them aren't carrying weapons," Mia confirmed.

"Isn't it strange that they have no fighters to protect their villages?" Joran asked. "Especially considering we're at war."

Alexandra shrugged, seeming indifferent to his observation. "Perhaps they assumed their magic would protect them. It would have too, if not for your help. They wouldn't be the first foe to fall after underestimating the empire's power."

Joran had his doubts, but didn't want to argue.

The soldiers finally reached the ground and formed up. They marched through the village slaughtering anyone that got in their way. It didn't take long for Joran to get his fill and retreat to his couch.

"War is ugly," Mia said as she sat beside him. "The quicker we end it and force the natives to accept the empire, the better for everyone."

"Somehow I doubt the lizardmen would agree." Joran forced his distaste for the killing aside. Given his new position, he figured he'd do well to get used to death.

Half an hour later the drop troops gave the all-clear signal. Alexandra spun away from the window and strode toward the rear of the bridge. "Come on. Time to see what we can learn."

"Down there?" Joran shuddered at the thought.

"Relax," Alexandra said. "We have a gondola that will lower us. You won't have to hang on to the ropes the way the drop troops do."

If getting down there turned out to be the worst part of the job, Joran would be both surprised and pleased.

———

Riding the gondola down to the village turned out not to be, by a long shot, the worst part. The stink hit Joran first. Somehow he'd expected it to take longer to reek this badly. Perhaps lizardmen rotted faster than humans. The bodies of dead lizardmen lay scattered about like so much litter—bloody, broken litter. Little distinguished males from females, but the dozen or so half-sized ones forced him to look away. Slaughtering their young struck Joran as a poor strategy to win the natives over to the empire's side.

On the other hand, the lizardmen hadn't been overly discriminating when they attacked Cularo, so maybe the killing of innocents in retribution made a certain amount of sense. Not that he liked it any better for all that.

He gave voice to none of his concerns. Alexandra looked around seeming well pleased. No doubt finally bringing the fight to the enemy relieved her greatly. Good thing someone was pleased. It took all Joran's self-control not to vomit.

A shrill shriek drew their attention just in time to see Knight Captain Antius run a squirming lizardman through the back. His white uniform and armor still gleamed as if the blood didn't dare stick to it lest it insult The One God.

In reality, Joran knew the exact alchemical compound the White Knights used to keep their uniforms spotless. Their souls, doubtless, were a mess.

Alexandra led the way over to one of the drop troopers. "Report."

"We faced no serious resistance, Majesty. As best I could tell there were only old and young males defending the village. As you commanded, we let several escape. My trackers are following them now."

"Good. Did you find anything that might tell us where the fighting-age males are?"

"No, but we haven't done a thorough search of the village yet."

"I'd say the area looks secure. How about you start that search?"

The drop trooper saluted. "As you command, Majesty."

One of the stone huts stood a little taller than the rest and sported a statue, crudely made, of some sort of figure.

"Mia and I will take this one," Joran said. "I believe it's a temple of some sort."

Alexandra waved him away and Joran set out for the structure.

"What makes you think it's a temple?" Mia asked.

"Given the size and its prominent position in the center of the village, it's either a temple or some sort of government building. Since we've seen nothing resembling a formal government, I guessed it was a temple. Perhaps I'm wrong, but we'll know for sure soon."

Outside the temple, Joran paused to study the statue. What he'd first taken to be a single figure turned out to be a pair of lizardmen carved from a single piece of stone. They had no real detail and no writing indicated who or what they were supposed to be.

His examination ended rather abruptly when Antius kicked the statue over, smashing it to pieces. "A heathen idol. No doubt depicting one of their demonic patrons. Best keep a close watch on your soul lest it be corrupted by these savages and their magic."

Joran had no idea how one went about keeping an eye on his soul, but he nodded and said, "Thank you for your concern, Knight Captain. Will you be joining us for the search inside?"

"I will not. Were it up to me, the cursed place would be cleansed with holy fire at once. Only Her Majesty's hope of finding a clue to the rest of the savages' hideout stays my hand. No follower of The One God should want to explore such a corrupt place."

He shot Joran a hard look before stalking off to find someone else to lecture.

Mia pushed the door open and Joran stepped inside. When it had closed behind her he said, "As missionaries go, the White Knights leave something to be desired."

Mia looked back as if fearing Antius might be standing

there listening. "They're good fighters. Their faith lets them keep going when anyone else would fall. You don't approve?"

Joran shrugged. "My approval or lack thereof is entirely irrelevant. The White Knights are what they are and have been for centuries. It often takes generations for the church's actual missionaries to undo the damage they cause the faith. Anyway, let's focus on the problem at hand."

A cool, blueish glow that seemed to have no particular origin filled the space. Much as he would have liked to figure out how the magic worked, Joran wouldn't dare try. The church considered any magic besides alchemy to be the work of demons. He had serious doubts about that as well, but he kept them buried deep down inside.

There were no benches or altar like you'd expect to find in a place of worship. The temple did have a raised space at the rear where an altar would have sat in a church of The One God. He figured if there was anything to find, that's where he'd find it.

His hopes were dashed when he reached the empty space and found nothing save a circle of smooth stone. Looked like Antius could burn the place whenever he wanted.

"Joran." Mia had broken off and moved to a spot about ten paces away. "Look at this."

He joined her and frowned at the markings someone had drawn on the blank stone with what he guessed was a charcoal stick. It looked like a crude, dark triangle flanked on either side by white figures that very much resembled the statue outside only separated by the mountain. He set his kit down and pulled out his notebook and pencil. It took only moments to duplicate the drawing.

"Do you take that everywhere with you?" Mia nodded toward his kit.

"Of course. An alchemist without his kit is pretty much useless. I would no more leave it behind than you would your sword."

He put the notebook away and they made a final circle around the room. Confident that they'd found the only item of interest, he led the way back outside. Barely a step away from the temple, a soldier burst from the jungle and ran over to Alexandra and the other commanders.

Curious, Joran went to join them.

"I lost the lizardman's trail about half a mile from here. Not sure if it took to the trees or what. The thing was headed dead north, toward the mountains. Unless it suddenly changed direction, that's got to be where the rest are hiding."

"Well done," Alexandra said. "If we can track down their exact position, we can bring in the rest of the legions and wipe them out."

"Did any of the mountains stand out to you?" Joran asked. Alexandra and the other commanders looked at him but he did his best not to pay attention.

"How do you mean, my lord?" the scout asked.

"Did any of them look dark? Or perhaps when you looked at it a chill went up your spine. Something like that?"

"Now that you mention it, I did see one kind of short, squatty mountain that looked darker than the rest, though I felt nothing especially supernatural about it."

"Thank you." He turned to Alexandra. "That will be the one you want to aim for."

"How do you know?" she asked.

"I found a drawing of something similar in the temple. It appears the natives regard the mountain as a sort of holy place." That observation drew a derisive snort from Antius. "At any rate, I think it's a good place to start."

"Then that's what we'll do." Alexandra drew a circle in the air with her finger. "Let's load up. Our hunt resumes."

"What about the village?" Antius asked. "It should be burned."

Alexandra turned to look at him. "It's a bunch of rock huts in the middle of a dirt field. What, exactly, do you plan to burn?"

He grumbled something and looked away.

"Exactly. We have more important uses for our supply of alchemist's fire." With that pronouncement she led the way back to the gondola. As they rode up to the dragon ship she muttered, "Bloody zealots."

Joran couldn't have agreed more, but he kept silent. An imperial princess might get away with saying things that a lesser noble dared not. And given Antius's fondness for fire, Joran determined it wise to stay on the man's good side.

Assuming he had one.

CHAPTER 17

Draq stood at the edge of the entrance to the holy cave, looking out over the warriors assembled in a clearing at the base of the mountain. Three hundred of his strongest tribesmen along with twelve runners had gathered to protect the holy place. They weren't the most impressive army in the history of the land, but he felt great pride in them nonetheless.

Voxel sat cross-legged beside him, eyes closed as he communed with the earth spirits. The shaman had offered little in the way of advice as they waited for the inevitable battle with the empire.

The few messengers he'd sent out to ask the other tribes for aid had yet to return and Draq held little hope for a positive reply even when they did get back. The tribes tended to handle their own problems and ignore anything outside their territory. The practice had served them well, keeping battles between tribes to a minimum over generations. Now, when they faced an enemy far too great for any one of them to handle, they had no plan to come together to fight the threat.

He hissed a sigh. As chieftain Draq respected and upheld tradition, but now that tradition threatened to get them all killed.

A hissing murmur ran through the assembled warriors when an adolescent male burst from the jungle at a full sprint. He ignored the others and went straight to Draq. The youth tried to speak, but his words came out as nothing more than wheezes.

"Steady, young one." Draq kept his voice calm but inside his soul trembled as he considered what might have brought this near child running in such a state. "Gather yourself and speak."

The young lizardman straightened and said, "My village has been destroyed by the humans. They killed everyone, even the hatchlings. I barely escaped to bring you a warning."

"You did well. Fear not, your village will be avenged. Go now and find food and water."

"When the humans come I want to fight." The youth's fierce request didn't surprise Draq. Losing everything had that effect on people.

"If it comes to battle, we will welcome your spear. Go now and rest. You'll be no good to us exhausted."

"That boy has no idea what he's asking for." Voxel opened his eyes and looked up at Draq.

"On the contrary, I suspect he knows exactly what he's asking for: a good death that takes some of those that killed his family and friends with him. I can't deny him that."

"All you grant him is a swift death." Voxel's gaze shifted to the sky. "They come."

In the distance Draq just made out three giant shapes turning right toward them. "They let him go so that he'd show them where to find us."

"Probably. Unfortunately for us, the humans aren't stupid. I will do what I can to convince the wind spirits they've enslaved to not bring them any closer."

"I'll alert Samaritan and the Holy Ones."

Draq ducked back inside and made the short walk to Samaritan's workshop. He found the human seated on a crude stool, eyes closed.

He didn't open his eyes when he said, "They're coming."

"How did you know?" Draq asked.

"Your conversation carried very well down the tunnel. I warned you to bring your mothers and young here."

"I know, but it was a calculated risk. There are still several villages that remain safe. If we can keep the fighting here, no matter what happens, some of our tribe will survive."

Samaritan snorted a laugh. "If you believe that, you have no understanding of what the empire is capable of. Unless your people submit utterly to them and the church, they will hunt down and kill you all. Either way, your existence will change forever. Unless we find the weapon in time."

"Will you find it in time?"

"I don't know. I'd hoped for at least a few more weeks. Now we have at most days. I'll check on the excavation."

"The Holy Ones need to be told."

"No, they don't. Until the weapon is found, they have no part to play. Under no circumstance can their safety be risked. Should they die, we'll have no hope."

Draq lowered his head a fraction. His earlier failure to heed Samaritan's warning had gotten many of his tribe killed. He would not make the same mistake again.

"We will hold them as long as we can."

"And we will dig with all our might. If the spirits are with us, the empire will never recover from what we unleash here."

Samaritan bobbed his head and shoulders in a traditional show of respect. "Fight well."

Draq withdrew and returned to ready his warriors for battle. Regardless of what they unleashed, he doubted his tribe would ever be the same either.

———

Joran clutched the arm of his couch as the dragon ship bucked and shuddered. Beside him Mia held on tight as well, making him feel better about his own anxiety. Less than an hour had passed since they left the destroyed village and the dark mountain lay a good ten miles in the distance. Despite the perfectly clear blue sky, the ship rocked as though buffeted by heavy winds.

In the center of the bridge, Alexandra glared at the captain. She had nothing to hold on to, but seemed steady enough for all that.

"What the hell is going on?" she demanded.

The captain repeated the question down one of the talking pipes. He had to hold his ear next to the opening to hear the response. Finally he shook his head and turned to Alexandra. "There's nothing wrong with the sails or balloon. It must be some magic of the lizardmen's. Flight control recommends we make a clearing and land."

"We're still ten miles away!"

"I'm sorry, Majesty," the captain said. "If we keep trying to fight whatever magic is resisting us, we risk losing the ships."

Alexandra looked like she wanted to run the man through. A few deep breaths seemed to calm her. "Very well. Retreat to the edge of the magical effect and deploy Joran's formula.

Hopefully we can find a clearing at least big enough to set one of the gondolas down."

They fell back a couple miles and the bucking stopped. Joran found he could breathe again, though not easily. Escaping a bomb only to end up knocked out of the sky by some enemy magic didn't appeal to him. At least that magic appeared to have limited range.

A barrel of hastily deployed Essence of Autumn revealed a modest clearing, certainly big enough for the troops to deploy. The whole process took only minutes then they were moving aside to allow the other dragon ships to deploy their own drop troops.

"Orders, Majesty?" the captain asked.

"Take us back to Cularo. We'll bring the Fifth Legion out. Four thousand soldiers should be enough to defeat a few hundred savages."

The dragon ship slowly turned to begin the trip back to the provincial capital. Alexandra scrubbed a hand across her face, turned, and crooked a finger at Joran. "We need to talk."

He swallowed the sudden lump in his throat and followed her out of the bridge and down to her cabin. Mia followed along behind, seemingly forgotten by Alexandra. Joran was glad to have her along, not just for moral support, but for her knowledge of combat and the army in general.

When the door closed Alexandra turned to face him. Her eyes looked dark and tired. The campaign was taking its toll on her, Joran could see that as clearly as he could see his own hand. They sooner they ended this business, the better for everyone.

"How do we stop it?" Alexandra asked.

Joran cocked his head, not entirely sure what she meant. "Stop what?"

"The magic! Whatever it is they're doing to stop our dragon ships. If knowledge of their spell spreads, one of our biggest advantages will be negated. Do you have any idea what that will mean for the army?"

He did have a rough idea what it would mean. Softening up enemy formations with alchemist's fire would be out as would attacking with drop troops from behind.

"I have no idea how to stop them. All alchemy can do is locate and identify sources of magical energy. Negating or even suppressing it is something even the greatest masters have never managed. The best advice I can offer is to kill the shaman casting the spell."

"Brilliant! I never would have thought of that. Unfortunately, there's an army between us and the shaman. Once we defeat the army, killing the shaman is an afterthought." She stalked over to a bolted-down couch and sat. "I need a drink."

"There, at least, I can help you." Joran shrugged out of his kit and made a quick search. "Here we are."

He pulled out a metal flask and handed it to her. Alexandra unscrewed it and took a sip. Her eyes widened. "You keep whiskey in your alchemy kit?"

He nodded. "It's surprising how many simple medical potions have some sort of alcohol as a base. I prefer to use whiskey. And sometimes you just need a drink."

She laughed and some of the tension seemed to flow out of her. After a final swallow, Alexandra handed the flask back. Joran took a sip of his own then offered it to Mia, who shook her head. He put the now-half-empty flask away and sealed up his kit.

"I'm sorry I don't have a better answer for you," Joran said. "Magic is just one of our enemies' advantages that we can't directly overcome. At least not yet."

"Why is it so difficult to deal with?" Mia asked. "I mean, alchemy has found a way to bring people back from the edge of death. Why does magic pose such an impossible challenge?"

"The primary challenge is that we, that is alchemists in general, don't understand how magic works. We understand the healing process and so can create potions to expedite it. But magic remains a total mystery. Even worse, the church actively discourages anyone from investigating the subject. They say it's all demon worship and thus risks corrupting the soul of anyone that learns about it."

"Do you believe that?" Alexandra asked.

"I don't know. Challenging church doctrine, even if you have irrefutable proof that it's wrong, is professional if not literal suicide. As I have no desire to speak at length with an inquisitor on the subject, I keep well clear of the subject."

"My advisor shows his wisdom again." Alexandra got a thoughtful look, like her mind had wandered a hundred miles away. "Nevertheless, the military might have to start doing that research, church rules be damned. At some point we're going to run into a magical force we can't overcome with imperial steel and numbers. We need to be ready."

The way she looked at him sent a chill up Joran's spine. First he needed to get an investigation unit vetted then she'd want him to break church doctrine to investigate magic. At this rate his title was going to be downgraded from imperial advisor to rotting corpse.

CHAPTER 18

Joran hardly believed what he saw when he, Mia, and Alexandra stepped out of the gondola. In the day and a half it took to ferry the entire Fifth Legion to the jungle, the soldiers on the ground had cut and cleared a huge opening and used the logs to build a crude fortification. Nothing like imperial steel axes to make short work of felling and limbing. The scent of fresh-cut wood lay over everything and Joran took a deep breath. That might be a scent worth trying to re-create, assuming he ever returned to his old life.

It looked like the start of a new town. In fact, once things settled down, this would be a perfect spot to set up a trading post. Assuming there were any natives left to trade with. He made a mental note to mention it to his father when he finally got a chance to write home.

Alexandra glowered at everything as if displeased with what she saw. Though far from a military man, Joran saw nothing that concerned him.

Speaking of military men, General Caius came swaggering

up, his crimson cloak billowing behind him. He seemed almost a different man from the nervous, sweating fellow Joran remembered from their first meeting. Not that he wasn't still sweating, the heat made that unavoidable, but in the field he seemed more confident.

The general beamed at Alexandra. "As you can see, Majesty, we've made great progress."

"What progress?" Alexandra demanded. "I brought you here to kill lizardmen not do civil engineering. Have there even been raids?"

Caius's smile curdled. "No. The cowardly savages are too scared to attack our position. In a few more days the fortress will be complete and we can march out to destroy the enemy."

"You think they're brave enough to attack the provincial capital with a hundred warriors but afraid to attack this?" She waved a disgusted hand at the crude walls and watchtowers. "Try to think a little more creatively. Why else might they not have attacked?"

The rolls of fat jiggled as his jaw worked. Joran had seen less attractive people in his life, though they'd been plague victims he was studying in the morgue.

"Maybe they're waiting for something?" Alexandra prompted when her patience broke. "Maybe their goal is to buy time for some evil magical ritual. That mountain clearly has some significance in their primitive religion. While you amuse yourself building a fort, they get closer to their plan becoming reality."

"We needed a strong fallback position." Caius's excuse sounded pitiful even to Joran.

"The enemy numbers at most a few hundred." Alexandra clenched her fists and Joran wondered if she planned to strike the general. "The Fifth Legion numbers four thousand. Half of them, hell a quarter, should have been enough to kill every lizardman between here and the mountain. Instead, you wait and weary them with pointless building."

"What…what would you have me do, Majesty?" The poor man trembled now in the face of Alexandra's wrath.

She took a step closer to him. "I would have you gather your forces and march out to do battle with our enemies. I would have you kill them all. And I would have you do it right now!"

Caius fled, bellowing orders and waving his arms. Joran actually felt kind of bad for him.

"Idiots. I'm surrounded by idiots." She glanced at Joran. "Present company excepted."

"Thank you, Majesty." Joran hesitated then said, "I do have a small suggestion. Have the dragon ships wait at the very edge of the magical disturbance. Should the shaman turn his spells on the Fifth, they might be free to approach and attack from above. At the very least it might make the spellcaster hesitate before using his magic on the legion."

"Ha!" She clapped him on the shoulder. "Excellent idea. We might as well get some use out of the damn things, even if it is a bluff."

She dispatched one of her guards to carry the message.

Joran frowned. "Aren't we going back up?"

He couldn't believe he'd just suggested that, but if there was one place he wanted to be less than on the dragon ship, it was on the ground during a battle.

"No, I want to be down here in case Caius screws up. I doubt it will come to that. Despite my complaints, he's a competent tactician. Wiping out such a small opposing force should pose no challenge for him."

Joran swallowed a grimace. He truly hoped Alexandra

knew what she was talking about. Unfortunately, since he'd arrived in this forsaken province, nothing had gone the way anyone thought it should.

———

D raq paced near the cave entrance. His force had gathered their weapons. Plenty of them carried spears tipped with steel taken from the crashed enemy ship. He'd seen how effective those spears were, but even so he held out no hope for his people should battle be the deciding factor. They simply didn't have the numbers to defeat the human army. But they would fight all the same, to the last person if necessary. Every second would give the diggers more time to find the weapon Samaritan promised.

He wanted very much to check once more on their human ally's progress, but his presence would do nothing to speed the digging and out here he might at least do some good. Besides, the last time he'd spoken to Samaritan, the human's distinct lack of optimism had depressed Draq's already poor mood. He bared his teeth and hissed. They would find the weapon in time. To think otherwise would make the deaths to come meaningless.

A skinny lizardman burst from the tree line and sprinted toward him. Draq knew the reason for the scout's return before the youth even had a chance to speak.

"They're coming," the scout said. "Thousands of humans, Chieftain. How can we stop such an army?"

Draq didn't answer at once. The scout's panic worried him and he hoped it didn't spread to the rest of the fighters. At last he said in a voice loud enough to be heard by all the gathered warriors, "We don't have to defeat them. We only need to hold them back a little longer. The Holy Ones will awaken the hidden weapon and when they do, it will destroy the human army along with all of those in their walled city. Have faith and remember, you fight for not only yourself, but all your family and friends still waiting in the villages."

The warriors roared and thrust their stolen spears in the air. Good. They hadn't lost the will to fight.

"If you wish to fight," Draq said to the scout. "Take your place with the others. If not, there's no shame in fleeing."

"I will fight, Chieftain." The youngster hurried to join the others.

Draq shook his head. Had he just sent the youth to his death? He hated to think about it, but feared the answer was yes.

"You do what you must," Voxel said. "No more, no less."

Draq hissed a long sigh. "Perhaps, but that makes it no easier. Will the spirits aid us?"

"I can't attack the enemy army unless you wish me to release the spell keeping the flying ships away."

"No, if we're attacked from above as well, we'll be wiped out even faster." Draq wished their second shaman hadn't gotten himself killed. He also wished for a couple thousand more fighters. It seemed this wasn't his day for getting his wishes granted. "If it looks like we're about to be defeated, do what you can, but until then, keep the flying ships away."

"As you wish." Voxel returned to his meditation. Draq trusted his old friend to know what needed to be done and do it.

"Draq."

He snapped around when Samaritan spoke from the cave entrance. "Tell me you've found it."

The human shook his head. "Not yet, but I'm sure we're

close. I'm going to check right now. But first I wanted to give you these."

Draq hadn't noticed the wooden tray in Samaritan's hands. It held two dozen of the explosive vials like those used in the raid.

"I wish I'd had the time and resources to make more," Samaritan said. "Even so, they should help break up the legion's formation. That will buy you a few extra minutes."

A few extra minutes. Hearing the duration of his remaining life spoken of in such terms helped the desperation of his situation fully sink in.

"We will buy every second we can. I doubt we will speak again," Draq said. "So let me thank you for all you've done for my people, even if it ends up not being enough."

"The empire will fall." Samaritan shifted, giving Draq a look at his shadowed face. The human's eyes burned with such hate that Draq nearly took a step back before remembering that it wasn't directed at him. "If not this day, then another."

Samaritan spun, his dirty white cloak swirling around him, and retreated back into the mountain.

"That human gives me chills," Voxel said.

A vibration ran through the ground and the trees near the base of the mountain trembled. The human army had arrived. That gave Draq chills.

Included in the long list of things Joran never wanted to do, watching a war up close, even a small one, sat near the top. Yet here he found himself, standing at the edge of the tree line beside Alexandra and Mia, surrounded by Iron Guards, and watching the Fifth Legion marching toward a gathering of lizardmen that looked far too small to last more than five minutes.

The front row of soldiers locked their shields as they marched. Behind them, the others placed their shields over the heads of the row in front of them creating a turtle formation. If the imperial legions had an iconic formation, this had to be it.

Though the battle appeared to be a forgone conclusion, the cave behind the lizardmen drew Joran's eye. Something about the dark opening struck him as odd even though he couldn't say exactly why.

He turned to Mia. "Do you think you can throw a rock as far as that cave?"

She stared at him as if not fully comprehending the question. Understandable given the situation as it seemed totally unrelated to the battle about to begin.

"Maybe," she said at last. "It'll be a stretch. Why?"

"I want to see if there's magic in the area. I thought if I tied a pouch of revealing powder to a rock, when it hit we'd see if anything sparked."

Alexandra glared at them. "Will you two shut up? I'm trying to concentrate."

He didn't know what required such intense focus. The soldiers' backs blocked everything save the heads of the tallest lizardmen.

Joran shrugged and he and Mia moved a little ways away and when they did, the first explosion rocked the clearing. He looked over in time to see a handful of soldiers land in a heap, many of them in more than one piece.

The healer in him wanted to run out and try to help, but his sensible side said after the battle would be better.

Trying to blot out the tremendous clash of steel on steel

punctuated by an occasional blast, Joran quickly spotted a rock. He set his kit down and dug out a small pouch, the larger pouch of revealing powder, and a length of string.

"We're winning," Mia said as he tied his dust bomb together. "The legion is driving them back. I've never seen such a small force fight with more ferocity. If they had greater numbers, we might have been in trouble."

Joran nodded absently and tightened the last string. "See what you think."

She took the rock and hefted it. "The weight's good. I'll give it my best shot."

Mia took two quick strides and threw with all her might. The instant she released the stone, the earth trembled.

Joran ignored the distraction and kept his gaze locked on the stone. The trajectory looked good.

It hit and a puff of dust burst out right in front of the cave. As soon as it did, a nearly blinding flash of light filled the air.

Some insanely powerful magic had just been released.

———

Samaritan left his very brave and very doomed allies and made his way deeper into the cave. They had no time left. The miners needed to find the weapon now, before the empire broke through. He'd invested over a year on this project, six months of it in this wretched jungle. He refused to fail, not when victory was so close.

As if summoned by his desperate thought, one of the massively muscled diggers came running down the tunnel toward him. The giant lizardman wore only a loin cloth and even though Samaritan knew they couldn't sweat, he would have sworn his scales glistened.

"We found something," the digger said. "A light shines from a crack in the tunnel."

At last! This had to be it.

"Show me."

They hurried toward the dig, Samaritan moving so fast he practically dragged the miner along beside him. Soon enough a ruddy, hellish glow filled the tunnel.

The other miners stood well back from the tiny hole as if fearing what the light might do to them. Samaritan ignored the superstitious lizardmen and pressed his eye to the opening. The details weren't clear, but he felt certain the shaft lay beyond the thin wall.

Still, they had no time for further digging.

"Go and protect the cave entrance. I'll open the rest of the passage."

The miners needed no further prompting. They fled as if a demon pursued them.

Samaritan retreated as well, but only about fifteen feet. He pulled the final explosive vial from his satchel and hurled it at the wall.

The instant it left his fingers he leapt and pulled his cloak tight around him.

The explosion shook the tunnel.

Dust fell and rocks pummeled him. Bruising as it was, nothing got through his alchemically treated cloak. He allowed a few seconds for the dust to settle then hurried back up the tunnel. As he'd hoped, the path lay open. Beyond the shattered remains of the wall, he found a short ledge that led to a pit from which the ruddy, hellish light emerged.

Samaritan peered over the edge, but between the light and the shaft's depth, he saw nothing. Still, the pit perfectly matched the description he'd read during his research. The weapon had to be down there.

"Is it time?"

He spun to find the two white-scaled lizardmen standing just outside the entrance. The others called them Holy Ones, but Samaritan knew the truth, they were twins, and soul bound. That made them the key to unlocking the weapon. According to his research, only the sacrifice of a complete soul would rouse the weapon from its slumber.

"It is, Holy Ones. Are you prepared?"

A distant explosion punctuated the question. Sounded like the battle had gotten well and truly underway. That meant the lizardmen had only minutes to survive. The few explosive vials he'd provided would buy them seconds at most.

"We are. Our people die to give us this chance. We will not fail them."

"Then you know what you must do. May the spirits reward your sacrifice." He moved aside to let them pass.

They walked side by side in perfect unison to the edge of the pit and, after a final look into each other's eyes, jumped.

Samaritan didn't wait to see the result. He turned and ran.

He managed only a few strides before the whole mountain shook. A boulder fell from the ceiling, nearly crushing him. Instead of returning to his lab, Samaritan broke the opposite way. He had nothing vital to retrieve. In fact, he rather hoped someone found his lab. Let them see the lies the empire was built on.

He turned down a tunnel that led to a hidden exit on the far side of the mountain. While he hoped with all his soul that the weapon destroyed every imperial in the province, he had no intention of sticking around here to make sure.

Whatever happened, it would only be a blow to the enemy. A powerful one, he hoped. But surely not a fatal one. And he meant to see the entire stinking empire reduced to nothing.

CHAPTER 19

The blinding light had barely faded when Joran sprinted toward Alexandra, Mia right on his heels. He didn't know what sort of magic the natives had activated, but he'd never seen any reaction that powerful. He'd never even read about one and Joran had read most of the relevant books in the imperial library. They needed to go and they needed to go now.

"What the hell was that light?" Alexandra asked when he got close.

"Revealing powder." Joran skidded to a halt. "The natives just activated some sort of powerful magic. We need to flee. Back to the dragon ships and as far from the mountain as we can get before whatever they did fully activates."

"That's madness," Alexandra said. "We've won. Only a few survivors remain and they'll be dealt with in moments."

"Great. Then there's no need for us to remain." A faint tremor ran through the ground. That couldn't be a good sign. "Please, Alexandra, if you never listen to another word I say, listen to this. Something is going to happen and we do not want to be here when it does."

She looked at him and Joran did his best to look confident and slightly terrified. The latter took no acting at all.

"Very well. Messenger! Tell General Caius to finish up here and fall back to the defensive structure at best speed. And warn him that some enemy magic may be incoming." One of the Iron Guards saluted and sprinted for the general's command post at the rear of the legion. "Satisfied?"

Alexandra led the way back to the clearing at a pace far too slow to suit Joran.

Mia laid a hand on his shoulder. "Easy. Your anxiety won't get us there any faster."

Her touch calmed him at once. At least for a moment. Then another tremor, stronger than the last, rattled the ground. The trees shook, sending fronds falling all around them.

"Let's pick up the pace," Alexandra said.

Thank The One God.

The group broke into a jog. The path trampled down by the legion made for easy running at least.

By the time the fort appeared in front of them, the ground trembled constantly and a dull roar filled the air. Whatever was going to happen, Joran suspected it would happen soon.

"What's going on?" Alexandra asked.

"I don't know," Joran said. "But I fear we're all about to find out."

A crack opened in the earth and Alexandra shouted, "Get the gondola down here. We're leaving."

Lucky for them, Alexandra's dragon ship had remained stationed above the fort. The gondola hit the ground less than a minute after she gave the order and soon they were being hoisted up. Joran never would have believed he'd be so glad to get back into the sky.

Halfway up he looked back toward the dark mountain.

The top half exploded upward and a creature out of your worst nightmare appeared. It looked like a serpent, with a blunt head and scales black as midnight. Its eyes glowed with an inner fire as it scanned the area. The monster had to measure at least fifty yards long and it was bigger around than the balloon holding the dragon ship in the sky. And that was just what Joran could see of the thing. Who knew how much remained underground?

"The One God be merciful," Alexandra whispered.

Joran wouldn't turn down The One God's mercy, but he feared they'd need far more than that.

They were nearly to the dragon ship when the serpent lunged out of the mountain and slithered toward the battle-field. It moved far faster than a creature that size should have.

"How do we defeat such a creature?" one of the Iron Guards asked.

No one had an answer as the gondola locked into place in the ship's hold. A different guard opened the door and Alexandra strode through. Joran hurried to follow, as much to get away from the huge opening in the floor as anything.

When they'd left the Iron Guards behind Alexandra said, "Tell me everything you know about that creature and how we might stop it."

"I've never seen or read anything about such a thing and I have no idea how we might kill it."

Alexandra shot him a narrow-eyed glare. "That is not the answer I was hoping for."

"I don't know what else to tell you," Joran said. "The truth is the truth. I doubt anyone has heard of a creature like this.

There might be something in the Forbidden Section of the library, but I, having no desire to end up strapped to a rack, have never visited that collection. Likely we'll have better luck getting information from either a lizardman prisoner, assuming we took any, or from searching the mountain itself."

"Why don't we just burn the blasted thing from the air?" Mia said. "The other two dragon ships have a full load of alchemist's fire, right?"

Joran and Alexandra looked at her and Mia flinched as if she feared they might hit her.

"Would that work?" Alexandra asked.

"I haven't the slightest idea," Joran said. He wished she'd stop asking him as it exposed a troubling vein of ignorance on his part. "But Mia's suggestion is worth a try, though I suggest that you tell the captains to stay as high as possible."

"We'll need to clear out the Fifth before we attack. Burning our own soldiers alive won't do at all." They stepped onto the bridge and Alexandra said, "Captain, take us up. I want to see what's happening with that monster."

The order went down the tube and soon they were rising. Joran's curiosity got the best of him and he joined Alexandra and Mia at the main window.

He wished he hadn't.

When they reached a height that allowed them to see the battlefield, all they saw were legionnaires being tossed into the air. One poor man had been impaled on the serpent's right fang. He looked tiny compared to the monstrous serpent. More worrisome, the fang had gone right through his imperial steel armor. That seemed impossible, but the facts were undeniable.

One group of soldiers attacked the serpent on either side, their swords just bouncing off its black scales. Most of the soldiers, sensibly in Joran's opinion, were fleeing as fast as possible toward the fort. Not that anyone in their right mind would imagine the newly built walls holding that creature back should it choose to strike.

Alexandra must have read his mind. "Tell the soldiers on the ground not to muster at the fort. They need to separate into squads and make their own way back to Cularo on foot. The smaller the group the better, that should make it harder for that thing to attack them."

Her message got relayed and the trio refocused on the serpent. It must have gotten annoyed by the soldiers attacking its flanks as it surged forward, grinding them into pulp under its body. That convinced the rest of those brave enough not to have run instantly to flee.

Good. Joran had no desire to see anyone else die.

The serpent had other ideas. As soon as the soldiers broke and fled, it slithered after them, snapping some off the ground and simply running others over. The trees did nothing to slow it down. Anything that got in its way ended up crushed.

"Order one of the dragon ships to attack from maximum altitude," Alexandra said. "Even if we can't kill it, maybe we can distract it enough to give the soldiers a chance to escape. We'll observe the attack then return to Cularo to prepare for a full evacuation. The sooner we get the civilians out of danger, the better."

"What about the legions?" Mia asked.

"They will withdraw as well. Until we can figure out how to stop the serpent, I won't put them in harm's way."

Joran let out a breath. Alexandra's answer relieved some of his anxiety. He'd feared for a moment she might insist on taking the fight to the serpent despite its seeming invulnerability to imperial steel. That would have been the largest act of mass suicide in the empire's history.

It felt like everyone on the bridge held their breath as the other dragon ship flew closer to the rampaging serpent. At least it had been a minute or two since he saw it devour any soldiers. Joran dared hope the rest of the Fifth had cleared the area.

For its part, the serpent seemed to be destroying everything around it. Trees flew as it swung its tail left and right. It slithered around smashing the jungle to bits. There seemed to be no point beyond mindless destruction.

Then it focused on the approaching dragon ship. The vessel had to be several thousand feet above the ground, but the serpent still glared as though its angry gaze might be enough to bring the ship down. And maybe it would be. Joran still had no idea about the creature's limitations or abilities.

An orange glow appeared around the ship's dragon cannons and a moment later two rivers of alchemist's fire came pouring down.

They made a direct hit, splashing over the serpent's head and running down its back.

If the hellish flames caused the serpent any pain it gave no sign. Instead it bent down and snapped a massive tree out by the roots.

"Oh no," Joran said.

The serpent flung its head up, releasing the tree as it did.

The trunk soared up toward the dragon ship.

Despite the captain's best effort to dodge, the trunk still impacted. The ship's keel snapped and it started to collapse.

The ship broke in half and tiny figures poured out. The serpent slithered over and bit the men out of the air, swallowing them whole.

"Get us out of here," Alexandra said. "And order the remaining ship to join us. I'll not risk another attack on that thing."

"I'm sorry, Majesty," Mia said. "I never would—"

Alexandra raised a hand, cutting her off mid-apology. "I would have done it even if you said nothing. The fault lies with me and no other."

"No," Joran said. "The fault lies with that creature. And one way or another we will see it brought down."

"Yes, we will." Alexandra's smile was fierce.

Now they just needed to figure out how to do it.

CHAPTER 20

They reached Cularo without incident, thank The One God. Joran had been trying to come up with a plan to kill the giant serpent for the entire flight, but nothing occurred to him, at least nothing he thought had an actual chance of success. Its size made any sort of conventional weapon useless and its scales had proven themselves invulnerable to imperial steel. It shrugged off alchemist's fire as easily as a duck did water. Joran failed to imagine how anything could do that. The flames were the most destructive force in the imperial arsenal as far as Joran knew.

No, he'd have to think far outside convention if he hoped to find a solution. Of course, he really needed more information about what they faced. Somehow, he had to get around the creature and into that cave.

Joran shuddered at the thought. How had he gone from not wanting to leave his lab in Tiber to thinking about avoiding a giant serpent long enough to explore a no-doubt cursed mountain? Assuming he lived through the current crisis, he'd never have to listen to his father talk about adventures again.

They set down in the landing area of Cularo's government building. He shook his head and got up off his couch on the bridge. He was even getting used to flying in the dragon ships. Perhaps he'd hit his head and not realized it.

"Your mind is all over the place," Mia said. "Have you come up with any good ideas?"

"No, my ideas all stink. What about you?"

She chuckled. "I'm so out of my element I don't know what to think. I never dreamed such a monster might exist. The only plan I've come up with is to run as far and as fast as possible away from it."

"Were we on our own, I'd like that plan very much. Unfortunately, there are thousands of lives on the line and I fear we are the ones best suited to finding a potential solution."

"Come on, you two." Alexandra strode toward the exit. "The generals will be waiting and the sooner we get people on the road, the better."

Joran and Mia fell in behind her followed by the Iron Guards.

As they walked Joran asked, "Do you have any thoughts, Majesty?"

"Yes, all of them bad. I can handle planning a large-scale battle against conventional enemies, but that thing? It's like trying to fight a natural disaster with a sword; it doesn't work. What I can't figure out is how a bunch of savages like the lizardmen even knew it was there much less how to wake it up."

They stepped out into the courtyard and turned toward the castle. The stone structure had seemed much more impressive before he saw the serpent. Joran doubted it would last five seconds should the creature decide to destroy it.

"I hesitate to say this and certainly wouldn't in the presence of Knight Captain Antius, but when it comes to magic, the lizardmen doubtless know more about it than we do. So many avenues of research have been cut off due to the church that we're largely operating blind."

"Bloody zealots," Alexandra muttered. "I really need to speak with Father about this when we get back. In the meantime, we'll just have to muddle through as best we can. Any suggestions you have would be welcome."

In for a penny, in for a pound. "I need to get back to the cave. There must be something there, some clue that can help us defeat this thing."

"You'll have to go on foot. A dragon ship is likely to draw the serpent's attention and as it so ably demonstrated, we can't get high enough to stay safe. Join me at the meeting then you can get underway."

"I'll gather weapons and supplies," Mia said.

Alexandra dismissed her with a wave and she headed for the armory. Joran considered what he might need for alchemy supplies, but since he'd stocked up at Fort Adana, he hadn't used anything save a little revealing powder, so he should be set. He watched his soulmate's rapidly vanishing back and wished he could have gone with her.

Inside the castle Alexandra turned immediately toward the meeting room where he'd first met the various generals and commanders.

"What, exactly, do you wish me to say?" he asked.

"Nothing, unless someone asks you a question. In that case, answer honestly. The generals will be even more useless than usual if we keep secrets from them. Mostly I want you to listen then tell me your impressions afterwards."

Joran nodded though he didn't really see the point. None of them even knew the situation and he doubted they'd have anything useful to say about the serpent since they hadn't even seen the thing yet. He envied them that. The monster would doubtlessly haunt his dreams for years.

Everyone sat in the same place as last time save General Caius who doubtless had the misfortune to either be running through the jungle for his life or being digested by the serpent. Joran bet on the former as the general had been far enough to the rear to have plenty of time to flee.

"Gentlemen," Alexandra said. "A new threat has appeared."

She told them everything that happened, leaving nothing out as she did. The generals stared at her with slack-jawed expressions. Antius alone appeared feverish with holy zeal. The fool probably imagined some demonic serpent whose death would catapult him higher into the ranks of the church. He might well be right about the demonic part. The serpent certainly had little natural about it.

"What about Caius?" asked General Vitalio, commander of the Sixth Legion.

"No idea," Alexandra said. "We have to operate on the assumption that the Fifth will be lost to the final man. I hope I'm wrong, but the serpent makes me think otherwise."

"What's our plan of attack?" General Ventor asked.

"We have none. The army has no weapons capable of harming it. My plan is to abandon Cularo and flee north with the civilians. The more distance we put between us and the serpent, the more time we'll have to think up a strategy. To that end, Joran and Mia will be traveling back to the mountain to try and determine how the natives summoned it and whether it has any weaknesses."

When she said it out loud, the idea sounded even less sane than when Joran suggested it.

"It's perfectly obvious where the creature came from,"

Antius said. "The demon-worshipping savages must have summoned it from hell. Only the divine might of the church can send it back."

Alexandra nodded, seeming willing to humor the lunatic. "Excellent. How will the church manage this miracle?"

Antius sputtered a moment. "We'll need to contact His Holiness the Pope. Surely some divine inspiration will show us the way."

"Surely," Alexandra said. "In fact, I'd like you to take one of the dragon ships back to the capital and plead for his intervention. The sooner the Holy Father can resolve this matter, the more lives will be saved."

Antius cleared his throat. "No, I will send a messenger to Tiber with the news, but someone who understands the nature of demons must go to the mountain with your agents. I will see to that myself. The uninitiated may be deceived by the savages' infernal magics."

Joran's heart sank. Not only did he need to avoid the serpent, but now he'd have to deal with Antius and his madness. He didn't think the task before him could have gotten any harder, but it seemed he'd been overly optimistic.

"The smaller the group, the less likely they are to be noticed," Alexandra said. "Better if you remain behind."

He wanted to hug Alexandra just then.

"One person more or less is unlikely to draw the demon and my presence at the mountain will be vital. Only a member of the church will have the strength of will to overcome the unholy magic likely to be present. For the good of the empire, I must go."

Seeing Antius's face twisted in determination, Joran knew nothing Alexandra said—maybe not even a direct order if the

White Knight saw it as contradicting the duty of his faith—
would dissuade him.

Alexandra must have seen it too. She nodded a fraction.
"Very well. The empire thanks you for your devotion. Can you
be ready to depart in one hour?"

"I'm ready now." Antius leapt to his feet. "Why delay?"

"Supplies must be gathered, a route laid out, and numerous
other details decided upon." Alexandra turned to the rest of the
generals. "Ready your troops then send criers out into the city.
The evacuation begins at first light. Joran, come with me."

She stood and the generals joined her to bow as she
departed. Joran followed her out of the conference room and
upstairs to her suite. Once the door had closed, she blew out a
long sigh. "Sorry about Antius. I debated ordering him to stay,
but that's not a fight I care to have just now. Can you work
around him?"

"Certainly, though I'd prefer not to have to. The trick will
be if we encounter any lizardmen. I'd like to try and talk to
them, but I assume Antius will attack first and ask questions
later."

"A safe assumption." Alexandra licked her lips and glanced
at the servants, who kept their distance. "If you need to knock
him over the head and bury his body in a shallow grave, he will
not be missed."

Joran winced. "I appreciate your understanding, but I
would prefer it not come to that. In fact, if there's danger, his
sword might come in handy. If you have no other orders, I
should find Mia and let her know that we need food for an
extra person."

"No, you'll have to do what you think best. I'll have a dragon
ship on standby. You have flares in your kit, right?" When he

nodded she continued. "Fire one and they'll come pick you up as long as you're well away from the serpent. We'll be counting on you to figure out how to stop that thing. Should we fail, The One God alone knows where the serpent will end its rampage."

A giant serpent, a religious fanatic, and the fate of the empire on his and Mia's shoulders. If this didn't count as an adventure, he didn't know what did.

———

After his conversation with Alexandra, Joran had gone to join Mia in the armory. She took the news that Antius would be joining them on their journey far better than Joran had. Through their link he knew she hadn't even faked her indifference. She just shrugged and led the way to the storage area where she packed another bag with food as well as a tarp to make a shelter.

Joran figured they'd need at least three days to walk back to the mountain, so that meant two nights of camping in the wild at least.

He shuddered. If the roadside inns had been uncomfortable, the thought of sleeping on the ground left his whole body aching. How he longed for his feather bed back in Tiber. At least he had plenty of insect repellent in his kit. He might even share it with Antius, assuming his faith didn't turn the mosquitoes away all by itself.

Mia put a final oilskin pouch of jerky in a pack, tied it tight, and tossed it to Joran. "That's it. Where are we meeting our traveling companion?"

"He didn't say." Joran shrugged on the pack. It weighed considerably less than his kit and he suspected Mia had loaded it light, bless her. "I assume we'll find His Holiness near the castle gate."

"You should be careful what you say. Some of the more devout might consider your words blasphemy."

Mia led the way across the bustling courtyard. It seemed the legions were already mustering out. Good. The sooner they got underway the better.

Antius's white uniform made him stand out as he waited for them near the main gate. His foot tapped and he frowned even more deeply than usual. Joran kept his mouth shut as they neared and Mia held out the third pack without comment.

"Finally." Antius slipped the pack over his shoulders. "The One God's holy mission must not be delayed."

Joran gestured at the gate and said with as much respect as he could muster, "After you, Knight Captain."

Antius strode out at a brisk pace, head up and shoulders back, seemingly unaware of Joran's disdain. Or more likely indifferent to it. Joran glanced at Mia and rolled his eyes, drawing a faint smile.

The city buzzed with every bit as much activity as the keep. Merchants hastened to load wagons with as many valuables as possible while families did the same with their meager possessions. Luckily for everyone, few people had made the move to Cularo. There were at most four hundred civilians and probably less after the lizardmen attacked earlier.

Halfway to the city gates Joran spotted a solitary man with massive shoulders and a leather apron struggling to wrestle an anvil into the back of a two-wheeled cart. Was this the man Joran needed to speak with?

He hurried over and gave the anvil a shove into place. The blacksmith wiped sweat from his brow. "Much obliged, sir."

"Joran, and you're very welcome." He took a breath. There

really was no easy way to do this. "Were you expecting your wife and son to join you in the near future?"

"Yes, sir. They must have been delayed, thank The One God. This is no place for a woman and child."

Joran swallowed the lump in his throat and told him about the attack. The moment the smith's heart broke showed clearly on his broad, open face. He fell to his knees, weeping.

At this point Antius finally noticed he'd stopped and turned back to join him and Mia. "What is the problem? Our mission will not keep."

"It will keep a few more minutes." Joran knelt beside the bereft smith. "I am so very sorry for your loss. In the brief time I knew them, I grew to like them. Especially your son. He was a bright, inquisitive boy. You have my deepest apologies for not finding you sooner."

The smith looked up with red, swollen eyes. "No, sir. I thank you for your kindness. That you would take the time to speak to me with all this going on is more than I had reason to hope for. The One God's blessing on you."

"And on you," Joran said.

"So say we all," Mia added.

To his surprise Antius made a circle over his heart and murmured, "So say we all."

Joran finally stood. "I have to go. But should you make it to the next settlement, find a Den Cade trading post and tell them Joran Den Cade said you were to get whatever help you needed. We can always use a skilled smith."

"Thank you, my lord."

Joran gave him a final squeeze on the shoulder and the three of them resumed their journey to the city gates. As they walked Antius looked at him. "A horrible tragedy. We will make the savages pay for their crimes. Once we've sent their demon serpent back to hell, the rest of the lizardmen will be dealt with once and for all. There's no way the heathens will ever be fit to join the empire."

Joran just nodded, not trusting himself to speak. Despite needing to do it, Joran had never done anything so painful. At least now, if he died, he did so with that weight off his shoulders.

CHAPTER 21

Two and a half days of steady walking brought Joran and his companions within sight of the mountain. They'd caught glimpses of the serpent a few times in the distance as it thrashed through the jungle, smashing trees and generally laying waste to the landscape. If it had a purpose, Joran had yet to deduce what it might be. At least they hadn't come across any dead or wounded legionnaires. Whether that meant they were safe or had been eaten, he preferred not to know.

Antius had turned out to be a stoic companion, offering no complaints about either the sleeping arrangements or the food. Not that the man ate or slept that much. He seemed to keep going mainly on faith as he muttered prayers pretty much nonstop and occasionally looked skyward as if seeking divine inspiration. If he got any, he chose not to share it with Joran and Mia.

"Not far now," Mia said when they paused for a break around midmorning. "I can smell the bodies rotting."

Joran grimaced and tried to take shallow breaths.

"Do not worry," Antius said. "Their souls are with The One God. Their suffering is over."

He sounded jealous.

What concerned Joran was the serpent deciding to return. Not that it had shown much inclination to. As far as he could tell, it appeared to be gradually smashing its way toward Cularo. Hopefully at a slow enough pace that Alexandra would have plenty of time to get everyone away before it arrived.

Soon enough they were moving again. Another hour should bring them to the cave. Joran wanted to get there with plenty of daylight left. Walking through a battlefield in the sunlight would be bad enough. He really didn't want to have to do so at night.

An hour later they stepped out of the edge of the jungle and stared out over the ruined land. Bodies of humans and lizardmen littered the ground, many of them barely recognizable. The serpent made no distinction between the two sides which begged the question: did the lizardmen even realize what they'd unleashed? The more he saw, the more doubts he held.

"Heathen monster!" Antius ripped his sword from its sheath and sprinted away from them.

Joran finally noticed what got him so riled up. A single lizardman limped through the bodies. One arm hung useless at his side and blood ran down his torso.

"Antius! Stop!" This was their chance to get some real information, assuming the White Knight didn't cut him down.

Sensing his need, Mia sprinted after Antius at near-blinding speed.

For his part, the lizardman watched death approach with seeming disinterest. Perhaps he'd seen so much death it no longer scared him.

By some miracle Mia got there in time to block Antius's first blow.

"You dare interfere with my holy work?" Antius ground his teeth and pressed harder.

With her strength enhanced by their soul bond, Mia held her own despite the difference in size. "He's wounded and unarmed. We need answers, not another body."

"Anything the savage told you would be a self-serving lie. He's a demon-worshipping heathen monster and so must die."

Joran finally reached the pair, an open vial in his hand. "Antius!"

The White Knight looked at him and Joran blew across the vial, sending a fine vapor into Antius's face. He blinked twice and collapsed, unable to move from the neck down.

"He's going to be furious when that wears off." Mia sheathed her sword.

Joran corked the vial and swapped it for another which he drank. "No doubt, but as I said, we need information and it's damnably difficult to get it from a corpse."

He turned to the lizardman who hadn't moved during the confrontation. "Can you understand me? My name is Joran and I'm trying to figure out how to stop the serpent."

"I understand you, human," the lizardman said. "But I don't know how to stop the weapon and if I did, I wouldn't tell you."

The lizardman's words sounded like the imperial trade tongue in Joran's head and he also knew the words held only the truth. Good, that meant the potion worked as it should.

"What's your name?" he asked.

The lizardman drew back its lips revealing a set of sharp teeth. Mia shifted a fraction, ready to defend him if necessary. A fact that made Joran feel much better about his position.

"Please, I mean you no harm. Surely the serpent is as big a

threat to your people as mine. The monster appears to have no desire beyond mindless destruction."

"Much like your empire. I am Draq and I led these brave warriors against your soldiers. Everyone else died. I've been searching for survivors despite knowing what I'll find."

"Why did you fight us? Not now, but since the beginning when peaceful contact remained possible. We never had a chance to find a path to trade and coexistence."

"We were warned by one like him." Draq gave Antius a disgusted look.

"Lying savage!" Antius shouted and glared as if he could kill with only force of will. "The White Knights are the most holy servants of The One God's church. None of us would stoop to working with the likes of you."

"I apologize for Antius," Joran said. "He's not a bad man, just stubborn. When you say one like him, you mean a human dressed in white?"

"Yes. Though his cloak was caked with dirt and his face had scars he took great pains to hide. He said the empire was coming and that you would destroy our way of life if we didn't stop you."

Joran shook his head. "This man you spoke to twisted the truth. Yes, your lives would have changed under imperial rule, but for the better. Trade would have flourished. We would have brought healing and advanced farming techniques. Your people would have been wealthy and safe as provincial citizens."

"I smell no lie from you, human."

"Joran."

"Joran. Why would Samaritan—that's what he called himself—twist the truth to force us into a fight we couldn't win without the weapon?"

"Likely he wanted to summon the serpent and saw you and your people as a means to that end. My suspicion is that this Samaritan holds some grudge against the empire. For what, I have no idea." Joran glanced at Antius. "You're awfully quiet all of a sudden. Does the name Samaritan mean something to you?"

"No, but if this man manipulated the lizardmen into fighting us, he's responsible for the deaths of thousands. We will find him and bring him to justice. And perhaps peace between our peoples will be possible after all."

Antius had lied about not recognizing the name, but to Joran's surprise, he meant what he said about peace.

He turned back to Draq. "Will you help us stop the serpent before anyone else dies?"

"I know little enough, but if there's any hope for peace, I will do what I can. My people deserve that at least." Draq blew out a hissing sigh. "You are not what Samaritan said you'd be. I expected monsters, but you're just people."

Joran smiled. "I feel much the same way about you and little is considerably more than we know now. Please, tell us your story."

CHAPTER 22

D raq watched from the jungle shadows as scores of humans worked to carve a wide, flat path out of the wilderness. Even from a distance the stink of their sweat reached him. He knew not their purpose, but he'd never seen so many of the pale-skinned outlanders in one place before. They weren't completely unknown to him of course. A stray human wandered through the jungle now and then, usually hunting and often ending up in the belly of one of the many predators that called the jungle home.

But something felt different now. Unfortunately Draq didn't know exactly what. As chieftain, it was his duty to figure out what the humans intended and more importantly what his people should do about it.

Why, he silently asked the spirits, had the humans chosen to trespass in his tribe's territory?

As usual, his silent pleas went unanswered. No great surprise since Draq wasn't a shaman. The spirits never spoke to him. His dear friend Voxel, a trained shaman of consider-able skill, claimed the spirits often didn't answer his questions either, but at least they usually answered his calls for power.

Well, whatever their purpose, as long as they did nothing to trouble Draq's people, he would leave them to it.

He turned and nearly slammed into a figure dressed in a filthy white cloak.

Draq leapt back and leveled his stone-tipped spear.

The human held his hands to the side, well clear of the sword dangling at his waist. "Calm yourself."

Somehow the human's words sounded like the clan tongue. Such a thing should not be, but Draq's ears didn't lie. He didn't lower his weapon but did ease his posture a fraction. "How do you speak our language?"

"That is a long tale and one I fear we have no time for. My name is Samaritan and I have come to bring you a warning. Those men you see, they serve the Tiberian Empire. When they finish the road, the legions will come. They will seize this land and dominate all those who live here. Your way of life will be destroyed."

Draq tried to peer closer at the human but the hood of his cloak cast his face in deep shadows. He caught a glimpse of red scars and burning, angry eyes, but little else.

"Why would you betray your own kind to warn me?"

"They are not my kind!" Samaritan checked to make sure his outburst hadn't been noticed by the nearby workers. He need not have worried. As far as Draq had noticed they had time only for their work. "The empire is a monster, a leviathan that will consume the world if it isn't stopped. I have made it my life's work to see that they are."

"If they are so powerful, what can we do to stop them?"

Samaritan's burning eyes bore into Draq's. "That's why I'm here. For the first time I have found a way to hurt them and drive them from your land. Hidden here, in a dark mountain, is a weapon of such power that nothing can stand against it. With your help we can activate the weapon and defeat the empire."

Draq's head spun. He smelled no lie from the frighteningly intense human, but what he suggested sounded like madness. That said, he needed to seriously consider the warning. Anything less would be an insult to his tribe.

"Will you speak to my advisors? The shamans will likely know of this dark mountain you describe."

"Of course. Anything I can do to prevent another people from being consumed by the empire, I will do."

"Then come. I will guide you to our village."

———

Draq and Voxel stood a few paces away from Samaritan who still spoke softly with Tuga, the tribe's second shaman. The human had laid out everything he claimed the empire would do to Draq's people in explicit terms. He claimed thousands of soldiers would descend on the jungle. That they'd seize the land and enslave everyone, killing any who resisted. Through it all he never gave off the scent Draq associated with lies. If he was telling the truth, then they were in deep trouble.

Out in the village, the rest of the tribe carried on as usual. His people trusted him to handle anything that came up and Draq felt that weight keenly.

"What do you think, old friend?" Draq asked.

"I don't know what to think. The human clearly believes everything he told us, but whether it's certain to happen or only a possibility I can't say. The spirits tell me nothing. In any case, it would be madness to dismiss the threat."

"Agreed. Do you recognize this dark mountain he spoke of?"

"Unfortunately. It can be only one place. North of here is a mountain inhabited by mad spirits. At least I think of them as mad. Perhaps I simply do not understand them as I should. In any case, that must be what he seeks."

Draq nodded and made his decision. "The three of us will have to go there and see what can be found."

Draq spotted movement and looked up in time to see the Holy Ones approaching Samaritan and Tuga. Their white scales gleamed in the sunlight and everyone bowed as they passed. He hurried over to hear the beginning of the conversation.

"An honor to meet you both." Samaritan bowed to the pair.

"We have never met a human before," the left Holy One said. "What brings you to our humble home?"

"I brought warning of a great evil about to descend on your tribe. A decision is being made about the next step."

The Holy Ones turned to look at Draq. "What have you decided, Chieftain?"

"Voxel knows of the place Samaritan seeks. We will go there and see what more can be learned. Once I know all I can, I will decide what must happen."

"Very wise," the right Holy One said. "When the time comes to depart, we will join you."

Everything in Draq screamed that they should not be exposed to danger, but he dared not defy the Holy Ones in front of the entire tribe. "We welcome your thoughts."

Though Draq led the tribe, the people worshipped the Holy Ones as emissaries of the spirits. He had to be very careful how he dealt with them. Showing less than the proper respect would see Draq removed as chieftain. That said, he dared not let them lead the tribe to ruin.

Voxel came to his rescue. "We should rest and depart at first light. Barring trouble, we can reach the mountain before nightfall."

Draq swallowed a sigh of relief. He had some time to think now. Hopefully he'd come up with some answers by morning.

———

The sun hung low in the sky when Draq and his party arrived in sight of the mountain. The stone looked darker than the rest of the peaks and it seemed to slump. Looking at it sent a chill down Draq's spine. He had a hard time imagining anything good coming from a place like this.

A hundred yards of open space separated the jungle from the base of the mountain. A slightly darker spot marked the location of a cave. That had to be where they were going.

"The spirits are thick here," the left Holy One said. "What do you make of it, Voxel?"

The shaman shook his head. "I don't know, Holy One. I can't understand the spirits that dwell in the mountain. Perhaps you will have better luck."

"We can but try," the right Holy One said.

For his part, Samaritan just stared at the mountain without comment.

"We'd best take a closer look," Draq said.

The human gave a full-body shake. "Yes. If this indeed is where the weapon was hidden, there should be signs inside."

At the base of the mountain, they found a narrow path leading up to the cave. The loose stone made the climbing difficult, but eventually everyone made it to the top. The light only reached about ten strides into the opening.

Voxel bent and picked up a fist-sized stone. The shaman closed his eyes and after a moment the stone began to glow. "Take this. I will remain here."

Draq accepted the stone and led the way into the cave. No danger presented itself, but his scales itched and any moment he expected something awful to happen. The Holy Ones looked around with rapt expressions. If they shared Draq's trepidation, they gave no sign.

For the first fifty strides the tunnel ran straight. One cave branched off but it held nothing save dust. Eventually the tunnel split left and right. Nothing distinguished one from the other.

Draq looked back at Samaritan. "Which way?"

"To the right," the Holy Ones answered in unison.

Draq had never heard them do that before. Taking it as a sign, they turned right and after a short walk entered a modest cavern as empty as the first chamber. The Holy Ones stared at the blank walls, clearly seeing something only visible to them.

"The spirits are thick here." The pair still spoke in perfect unison. "Whatever lies inside the mountain, they wish it to awaken. Fate brought us here, there can be no doubt. Return the way we came and you will find what you seek."

With that final pronouncement, the Holy Ones sat facing each other, eyes closed.

Draq looked at Samaritan who shrugged. They retreated back to the intersection and took the left-hand tunnel. It twisted and turned, slowly rising until it ended at a blank wall.

He raised the light for a better look.

"This is it!" Samaritan ran his hand over the wall like it was his lover's scales. "Do you see the mark? The ancient ones put it here to mark the weapon's location."

Draq looked closer. Some sort of faded mark covered a portion of the wall, but it meant nothing to him.

"So where is the weapon?" he asked.

"Beyond the seal. We'll need to dig until we reach it. Steel tools will be necessary."

Draq snorted. "Where do you expect us to get steel tools?"

He caught a hint of Samaritan's smile. "Have no fear. Where the legions go, the merchants follow. You will find one greedy and stupid enough to trade you everything we need to secure their destruction."

Draq didn't especially like it, but if the Holy Ones said the weapon had to be awakened, then his options were limited. It implied that the spirits agreed with Samaritan. For him to go against that would require more than personal discomfort with the decision.

"Very well. It seems we are going to war."

CHAPTER 23

Joran's mind raced as he considered the story Draq told him and he then repeated to his companions. It seemed impossible that anyone might hate the empire to such an extent that he would risk unleashing a creature like the serpent. Perhaps if he'd had some way to control who and where it attacked, but as far as Joran could tell, the beast acted as a force of pure destruction, as likely to slaughter ally as enemy.

He shook his head. They'd probably never know Samaritan's true intentions unless they caught up with the man and forced him to talk. Joran dearly hoped they did find him. Preferably before he wreaked any more havoc.

Draq ended his story and said, "We did everything in our power to delay you long enough for the diggers to reach the weapon. We succeeded after a fashion. Having seen the creature that we woke, I can't imagine that it will simply swing around our villages. And once it finishes with our territory, no doubt the other tribes will be in danger as well."

"Do you think Samaritan knew what he sought to unleash?" Joran asked.

"Perhaps, though he never called it anything save 'the weapon' when he spoke of it to us." Draq bared his fangs, his fury palpable. "He manipulated me, used my fear and ignorance to destroy his enemies. My tribe was nothing more than a tool to be used and cast aside when no longer of value. He may have done something to ensorcel the Holy Ones as well. Why else would they think the spirits told them to awaken a creature as likely to destroy their own people as yours?"

"I know nothing about spirits," Joran said. "But it occurs to me that what actually enchanted your Holy Ones was the serpent itself. If they were sensitive to magical energies, it might have reached out to compel them. That's just a guess on my part, of course. One last question. How did you know where and when Her Majesty's dragon ship would go down?"

"Samaritan told us. Sometimes he would take out this strange silver amulet and cock his head as if listening. Afterward he'd tell us something the empire had planned or something that would soon happen."

"Interesting, he must have had a way to communicate with the infiltrators."

"Enough discussion." Antius had regained his feet and seemed no worse for the light application of paralyzing powder. At least he made no effort to attack Draq again. "Let us see what secrets the cave holds."

"Excellent idea." Joran turned to Draq. "Will you join us?"

Draq shook his head. "I need to check on the other villages. I've told you all I know. Good luck, Joran."

Joran dug a vial filled with a pale-red liquid out of his kit and offered it to the lizardman. "I don't know how long a walk you have, but this will make it more comfortable."

Draq eyed the vial, his lips peeled back a fraction in what Joran suspected indicated distrust.

"If I wished you dead, I could have let Antius cut your head off. Please, it's a minor healing potion. It should seal your wounds enough that you won't get an infection at least, as well as numb the pain."

The lizardman at last took the vial, uncorked it, and threw the potion back. His narrow black eyes widened in surprise as the potion did its work. "A miracle worthy of the finest shamans. Clearly the spirits favor you, friend Joran. I hope we see one another again."

Joran smiled, pleased to have been upgraded to friend. "I hope so as well. I also hope your people come through this trial with no more losses."

Draq took his leave, moving easier now. When he'd slipped into the jungle, the little group climbed the narrow path up to the cave. Joran nearly fell on his face twice, but both times Mia caught his arm. He appreciated the save even if he did find it slightly embarrassing.

"Thanks," he said when they finally reached the cave mouth. "I'm not exactly used to this sort of thing."

Mia grinned. "No kidding. I don't know if this is normal, but I understood what Draq said before you translated for us. Like I heard the words on a slight delay."

"Perhaps our soul bond allowed you to share the effects of the potion. We'll have to experiment with that some-time, assuming we ever get a quiet day or two for ourselves." Joran took a step toward the cave and froze. "Ugh."

Four lizardmen had been crushed by falling rocks leaving the cave half sealed.

"Don't be so squeamish." Antius pulled himself up and over

the pile. "The rest of the tunnel looks clear, though I can't see very far."

Mia went next then reached back to help Joran. Much as he enjoyed the clarity of thought the soul bond brought him, a little of the physical enhancements would have been nice as well. He had a potion that would boost his strength and speed, but it had some nasty side effects and he preferred not to use it unless life and death were involved.

Once all three of them stood in the dark tunnel, Joran took yet another vial out of his kit and shook it until it glowed bright blue. The light revealed some huge boulders deeper in that must have fallen when the serpent burst out of the mountain. None of them made the tunnel impassable, so the group set out.

A few yards in Antius said, "I sense nothing demonic. Perhaps the serpent wasn't summoned from hell."

"Is that something White Knights learn to do?" Mia asked, genuine curiosity radiating through their link.

Antius looked away and Joran suspected if they could have seen his face it would have been red. "Well, no, but as a devout follower of The One God, surely I would know if something truly evil had lived here for a long time."

Joran kept his doubts to himself. Antius had already been proven wrong about the natives. Still, no reason to burst his bubble a second time.

It took them only a few minutes to reach the first side chamber. From Draq's description this had to be the room Samaritan used for his lab. Sure enough the light revealed a stone table covered with flasks, burners, and other alchemy tools. Over it all lay a coat of dirt that must have fallen from the ceiling during the tremor. It was a miracle nothing smashed the set to shards.

Joran moved closer, inspecting the layout. "This is textbook."

"What do you mean?" Antius joined him near the workbench.

"I mean the way this workstation is set up looks exactly the way a first-year alchemy textbook shows it. Samaritan must have trained at the imperial college for two years or less."

"Why only two years?" Mia asked.

"Because if he'd been at it longer than that, he would have found a setup that worked better for him than the one they teach beginners. I haven't used this layout in years. If we only knew how old he was, we'd be able to figure out when he attended the college. That would give us a rough idea where to start looking for his identity."

Antius gave him a hard glare. "You need not worry about this charlatan pretending to be a White Knight. The church will deal with him. Focus on finding a way to stop the serpent."

Looked like Joran touched a nerve. More than ever he felt certain Antius knew Samaritan's true identity. But a confrontation would have to wait. He'd report to Alexandra and let her decide the best course.

"Are you coming?" Antius asked from the tunnel.

"Yes, just a moment."

On the end of the workbench he spotted a dust-covered book. He brushed it off and flipped through the pages. It was Samaritan's work journal. Talk about a lucky break.

Joran made eye contact with Mia and touched a finger to his lips before slipping the book into his kit. He led her out into the tunnel and they set out once more. The deeper they went the more broken rock filled the passage. They had to be getting close to where the serpent emerged.

At the intersection they turned left and soon reached the spot where the lizardmen started digging.

"I wonder..." Joran muttered and dug a pouch of revealing powder out of his kit.

Ten yards ahead Antius turned back. "Now what? We're nearly there."

It seemed Antius had left his reasonable side out on the battlefield.

"This is an investigation, remember? We're not just hiking to the spot where the serpent emerged. We also need to figure out everything going on around it. I'm curious to see if there's some sort of magic at the start of the tunnel. Maybe some hint of how such a powerful creature ended up sealed in this mountain."

Antius grunted and crossed his arms. He seemed less than pleased, but at least he didn't complain anymore.

Joran sprinkled the revealing powder around the area and almost at once it started to glow. As more and more of the dust spread out, the glow outlined a shape.

"It looks like the serpent," Mia said.

"Yes. I suspect the marking served as a warning not to come any closer. Or in Samaritan's case as a confirmation that he'd found the right place. Would you hold my kit for a moment?"

Joran handed her the pack and removed his own journal as well as a charcoal stick. He quickly sketched the design for future research. That done, they joined the ever-impatient Antius in the tunnel. It went on for a dozen strides before exiting at a ledge. Sun shone down on them through the hole smashed in the mountain.

"This is where it came from." Antius glared around as if angry with the mountain for housing the creature.

Joran steeled himself and peeked over the edge. Heat

washed over his face and at the bottom he saw an angry red glow. "It's a lava pit. If the serpent lived in a pool of molten lava for The One God only knows how long, that certainly explains why alchemist's fire didn't hurt it."

"Then what will?" Mia asked.

"I wish I knew."

Antius threw up his hands. "This was a complete waste of time. We learned nothing useful save the identity of our true enemy. We still have no clue how to stop the serpent. Our time would have been better spent praying for divine inspiration."

"You can still pray if you like," Joran said. "I'm going back to the lab to see what else I can find."

He turned back and Mia fell in beside him. Unless he wanted to stand in the dark, Antius would be right behind them.

"Do you think there's anything else to find?" Mia asked

"If there isn't, I have no idea what we're going to do next besides pray with Antius."

A moment after they stepped into the lab, Antius went stomping past. Joran didn't particularly like the man, but he had no desire to leave him lost in the dark.

"What are we looking for?" Mia asked.

Joran shook his head. "I really don't know. It's unlikely Samaritan had a better supply of chemicals than I do considering the list Gris gave us. But if he had access to other things, we might get lucky. If you don't mind holding the light while I search, it might speed things up."

She smiled at his awkward request. "I'm not easily offended, especially when none is meant. And I wouldn't know what to look for anyway. Give me the light."

Joran handed her the glowing vial and shrugged out of his kit. A few hard puffs of air blew away most of the dust. Unfortunately none of the containers were marked. He picked up a flask and sniffed. A half-mixed explosive, nothing remotely strong enough to be of use.

Joran set it aside, carefully, and moved on. Forty-five minutes passed as he checked each container and came up empty. At last he picked up a final, nearly empty vial. It hadn't been part of the processing setup which made him hope Samaritan had brought it with him and forgot to collect it before he fled.

He sniffed and immediately jerked his head back. His head spun for a moment and he fought not to gag. Though he'd never encountered it personally, every alchemy student was taught about that stench. Only one substance combined the odor with a thick, tar-like liquid. Black Bile of the Earth, the most lethal substance on the planet and their best hope to kill the serpent.

Even as relief flooded through him, he couldn't help wondering where Samaritan had gotten his hands on such a rare and powerful poison. And of even more concern, did he have more?

CHAPTER 24

Joran emerged from the tunnel to find Antius on his knees, hands clasped in front of him, head bowed in prayer. When he'd said he planned to pray for guidance, Joran hadn't actually thought he meant right now. You had to respect the man's faith. Some people, and Joran included himself in this group, worshipped The One God because the empire required it more than from actual belief. As far as Joran was concerned, everything he'd accomplished came from hard work and determination rather than divine intervention.

"Joran." Mia pointed in the distance.

He turned to look. "Uh-oh."

The serpent had turned their way and was rapidly closing the distance. He didn't think they'd done anything to draw the creature's attention, but then again, if it involved magic, Joran wouldn't have even realized anything happened.

"Antius, we need to move."

"I am in the middle of my devotion. I waited while you searched, you will remain silent while I finish my prayer."

"The serpent's coming this way and unless you can pray it away, I suggest we be somewhere else when it arrives."

Antius finally opened his eyes, eyes that grew very wide indeed. He made a circle over his heart. "I can finish the prayer when we get back to Cularo."

The trio half slid half ran down to the base of the mountain before turning toward the jungle. Outrunning it didn't seem like an option, but maybe if they got out of sight, the monster would slither off somewhere else.

When they'd put a hundred yards or so between them and the mountain, Joran had to stop. His legs burned and his breathing sounded like a bellows with a hole in the side.

He leaned against a tree and watched through gaps in the leaves as the serpent crashed through a row of trees and entered the clearing. Its long, forked tongue shot out, tasting the air. The massive head swung back and forth before turning their way.

Antius opened his mouth. Mia immediately clamped her hand over it. Joran pointed at the serpent and shook his head.

Antius nodded and she let him go.

Now Joran threw a short prayer heavenward. When confronted by something out of your control, sometimes you had no other choice.

Maybe The One God heard or maybe they just got lucky, but on the opposite side of the clearing emerged a huge reptile creature like the one the shaman he and Mia fought rode. How the stupid thing failed to notice a serpent half the size of a mountain he didn't know or care.

As soon as the monster turned to strike, they fled, determined to put as much distance between themselves and the serpent as possible.

Ten minutes at a quick march had Joran exhausted again.

He had to pause for a rest. Antius gave him a disgusted look, but Mia offered a hand on his shoulder in support. Neither of them had the decency to be out of breath.

"Friend Joran."

He spun to find Draq a few paces away waving at them. While he had hoped to see the lizardman again, Joran didn't expect to do so this soon.

They hurried over and Joran said, "This is a surprise. I thought you were going to check on your people."

"I did, but soon found one of the warriors I left to protect the nearest village. They saw the serpent and fled to some caves we use as a refuge from time to time. He was out looking for stragglers. Once we spoke, I returned to see if I could help after all. When I spotted the serpent returning, I sought out the thunder beast to cause a distraction."

"You probably saved our lives." Joran clapped him on the shoulder, prompting the lizardman to cock his head in confusion. "Still, I'm surprised the beast would come this way with the serpent nearby."

"Thunder beasts are stupid. They're so big they can't imagine anything hurting them. Or so the shamans claim. Where do you need to go?"

Joran glanced back again. "About ten miles from wherever that thing is."

"Miles, yes, the human merchant used this term. Follow me, I will guide you along the fastest paths."

Joran doubted he had any fast left in him, but he set out again at a determined plod. If he tried to go any faster, he wouldn't need the serpent to eat him, he'd likely collapse all on his own.

Draq led them safely through the jungle along paths he claimed were known only to his tribe. All that interested Joran was the lack of obstacles to tangle his feet now that he could barely get them off the ground. When they finally reached a clearing with a view of the sky he nearly collapsed.

"The creature didn't follow us," Draq said. "I believe you will be safe here."

"Thanks." Joran unslung his kit and pulled out one of his two flares. If the dragon ship Alexandra promised kept watch, they should have no trouble retrieving them here. "Do you wish to come back with us?"

Draq shook his head, a surprisingly human action. "Until the threat is eliminated, I will stay with my people. Once matters are settled, come to the mountain. I will find you there."

"That's probably a good idea. Until I've spoken to our chieftain, it will be best for our people to keep their distance from each other. That said, I look forward to a calmer conversation in the future."

Draq made a little bobbing motion that suggested a bow and vanished into the jungle.

Now to make their own escape. Joran undid the string wrapped around the flare, pointed it skyward, and yanked. A spark activated a tiny explosive to send a three-inch-long tube soaring into the sky where it exploded with a golden light.

Lucky for them, the dragon ship noticed it before the serpent. Five minutes after setting off the flare, they were on their way up in a gondola. As soon as the crew finished securing the gondola, the ship turned to carry them north. It wouldn't take long to make the trip, but Joran planned to use every second to rest.

"I will complete my prayer." Antius stalked off. If the ship had a chapel, Joran didn't know about it.

He shrugged and went with Mia to the cabin they shared. Joran set his kit down and collapsed into his hammock. He felt so tired even Samaritan's workbook didn't tempt him.

"How will you trick the serpent into eating the poison?" Mia asked.

"Actually a spear tip smeared with the poison and stabbed into its mouth would be better. That will get it into the serpent's blood faster. Not that it should matter with Black Bile of the Earth. The amount left in that vial would suffice to kill everyone in Cularo with a bit left over. Unfortunately, its scales are so tough stabbing it anywhere else won't work."

"What about the eyes?"

"That might do it if you were fast enough, but I fear it would shut its eyelids before the spear hit. Plus the mouth is a bigger target and the thing isn't exactly shy about snapping at people. Anyway, that's Alexandra's problem. We did our part."

Mia chuckled. "You think she'll see it that way?"

"Probably not, but I can hope." Joran yawned. "Wake me when we start to land."

It seemed he'd barely closed his eyes when Mia's hand touched his shoulder. His eyes snapped open. "Already?"

"I waited until the last possible moment. You looked so peaceful I hated to do it, but we'll be tied up in minutes and I figured you'd need some time to wake up all the way."

"Yeah, thanks. Did you get any sleep?"

"I wasn't really tired."

Joran's lips twisted in a grimace of self-pity. Of course she wasn't. Running through the jungle didn't bother people in good shape. "Hear anything from Antius?"

"Not a thing. No doubt he spent the whole trip back praying."

Joran rolled out of his hammock. "Do you think he received any divine revelations?"

"I'm not optimistic."

He laughed. "Me neither. Come on."

With his kit once more over his shoulder, Joran followed Mia out of their cabin on down the stairs to the hold. At the bottom of the ramp they found Alexandra and her Iron Guards waiting. Toe tapping and arms crossed, she looked even less patient than usual.

"Please tell me you found something useful," she said.

Joran glanced around. They'd landed in the yard near the Cularo government building. He'd expected to find everyone gone already.

"We did find something useful, at least I assume it will be useful. With a creature like the serpent, who can be certain?"

"You'd better be. According to our spotters, the serpent has turned toward Cularo and is approaching fast. The civilians are gone, but they've managed less than a hundred miles. If we don't stop it here, it will catch them in a day or two."

"Well, here's my plan." Joran told her everything they'd found, ending with the poison. "Assuming we can pierce the flesh of its mouth, that should kill it in moments."

"What about using bait?" Alexandra asked. "We could strap the poison to Darsus and let the serpent eat him. Would that work?"

"Not as quickly, but yes, it should work. Assuming you can convince the serpent to eat him and not squash him like an ant. As far as I can tell, it's a coin flip whether it eats someone or pulps them and we've only got enough poison for one attempt.

Alexandra looked like she wanted to scream as she ran her fingers through her hair.

"I can do it, Majesty," Mia said. "Get me a spear and I'll see the beast slain."

"No." Joran's heart raced at the thought of anything happening to Mia. "It's too risky. Let someone else do it."

"I'm the fastest. You know that better than anyone. I have the best chance of surviving and there are too many lives on the line for anyone else to try."

He hated it, but knew she was right. "Then we do it together. If anything happens to you, there's no point in me living anyway."

She didn't try and argue. They both knew he'd spoken the simple truth.

Whether they lived or died, they'd do it together.

CHAPTER 25

The governor's compound had a proper alchemy lab tucked away in the back on the ground floor. Joran didn't know who set it up, but the room had a coat of dust nearly as thick as the chamber Samaritan used. Whoever looked after cleaning and maintenance clearly needed to find other employment. Fortunately, Joran only needed a small space and his own equipment.

Once he finished setting up, he tied a specially treated cloth across his mouth and nose. Prolonged exposure to the fumes from Black Bile could damage a person's lungs and he didn't want to risk it even for the few minutes it would take to extract the remaining poison.

Forcing himself to breathe and ignore the spicy scent of the treatment, Joran picked up the vial with a pair of padded tongs.

"Where do you think he got a sample of Black Bile of the Earth anyway?" Alexandra stood in the lab's doorway well away from the fumes.

The Iron Guards were a little less fussy in the mansion and at the moment it was just the two of them, Mia having gone to the armory to collect some other weapons. Assuming the spear Joran was getting ready to treat failed, he doubted anything she found would make a difference. But if it made her feel more prepared, he had no intention of complaining.

"I assume from outside the empire," Joran said. "The only source I know of is under imperial control and I can't imagine anyone raiding the fortress without word getting out. Since you've heard nothing…You haven't, right?"

"No."

"So there you go. Somewhere outside the empire. Beyond that, I have no idea. Now, no disrespect intended, but I really do need to concentrate."

"Of course. There will be time enough to investigate our many mysteries assuming we survive the serpent. Best of luck, Joran."

He glanced over his shoulder in time to see her slipping out of sight. With a shake of his head he put the princess out of his mind. The vial gripped firmly in his tongs, Joran used a long probe of imperial steel to coax out every drop of the thick black liquid. He applied it evenly along the tip and edge of the spear Mia had chosen as her primary weapon.

When he'd gotten everything possible, he gently fanned the coating until it hardened. Now it looked like the spearhead had a glittering black edge. The tiniest scratch would be instantly lethal. Hopefully to the serpent as well.

Finally, he slid the vial and prod into a specially treated bag and pulled it shut. Eventually they'd be buried at least ten feet deep and well away from any source of water. Something about being buried in the earth drained the negative effects of the poison, though according to the research he'd read it took several decades. Since the poison came from the earth that always struck him as strange, but as with many things that worked in alchemy, the precise reason why might never be known.

Putting the useless thoughts out of his mind, Joran left his kit behind and carried the spear outside. The servants had all evacuated with the other civilians and he encountered no soldiers during his brief walk. In the courtyard he found Mia waiting. She wore a fine new Iron Guard uniform, but no armor. Her sword hung at her left hip and it looked like she'd added a pair of daggers.

He took his mask off and handed her the spear. "It's as ready as it's going to get. Are you sure you want to go through with this?"

"Unless something's changed in the last hour, I don't think I have a choice. Better to face the serpent head on when we have a chance of winning."

"Okay. Where do you want to fight it?"

"I was thinking just inside the city wall. Her Majesty said to do whatever we had to in order to stop it and Cularo is pretty much empty. I figured if I had to retreat, the buildings would offer some cover."

"Don't count on it. That thing smashes trees like twigs, I doubt these little buildings will amount to much." They set out for Mia's preferred battlefield. "I do have a couple surprises ready should they prove necessary."

"You think you can hurt it?"

Joran shook his head. "Not a chance. I'm hoping I can distract it should you need to retreat. And even that's iffy."

They reached an open area within sight of the wall. In the distance, the serpent's head rose above the trees as it slithered ever closer. At the rate it approached, Joran figured they had at most five minutes. Not a ton of time left to live.

"We're not dying here." Mia hefted her spear. "I have every intention of meeting your parents when we get back to Tiber."

He couldn't help smiling. "Good luck. I'll be right here with you."

Joran moved to stand between two shops about a hundred feet away. Their link extended at least several hundred yards and probably more, but he wanted to stay close on the off chance he could be of some help.

Of course, if he had to help, they were probably doomed.

———

M ia shoved her fear into a little box in the back of her mind and while she was at it she shoved Joran's in there as well. Much as she appreciated his concern, the fear flooding their link did nothing to help her focus. Only cold confidence and determination would let her survive. And she intended to do exactly that. Dying a few weeks after meeting her soulmate would be too horrible.

Not that the giant serpent rapidly filling her vision cared about her good fortune. It looked at her with burning, soulless eyes. If it felt any emotions at all, doubtless they were all bad.

At last it towered over the wall and glared down at her. Its tongue flicked out and it swung its blunt head left and right. Perhaps it had hoped for more victims. It might even taste the nearby legions. The princess ordered them to hide out of sight so they didn't distract the serpent from the obvious target. Her.

"Hey! Come and get me, you overgrown garden snake." She brandished her spear and waved to get its attention.

The serpent seemed unimpressed with her goading and even Mia thought her insults needed work. She'd hoped the noise and movement would do the trick. Maybe that had been overly optimistic.

She sensed Joran's intention a moment before he stepped out from his hiding place, pointed something at the serpent, and yanked a string.

A flare shot out and slammed into its head before exploding in a blinding light. Before it dimmed, Joran had slipped back out of sight.

The serpent hissed and surged forward, smashing through the wall like it was nothing. Splinters flew everywhere, some of them nearly reaching Mia. If she got nothing worse than a splinter, she'd consider herself lucky.

It made no move to bite her.

Instead Mia threw herself to the side, barely avoiding getting crushed by the massive body. She also made sure to keep the spear's head well away from her. Joran must have warned her a dozen times about the danger of the black poison.

Barely back on her feet, the serpent twisted around to glare at her. Though she probably imagined it, she'd have sworn it looked angry, or angrier anyway.

"Come on! You can do better than that." Mia bared her own teeth as if that might coax it into opening its mouth.

She failed, but the serpent did act. It circled her, forming a wall of flesh that trapped her in a far-too-small circle.

No expert on snakes, Mia had never heard of a poisonous serpent crushing its victims. Of course, that was normal snakes. Somehow, she doubted the rules applied to this thing.

The circle closed as her mind raced for an escape route.

Something shattered and the serpent flinched before spinning around.

It appeared to have forgotten about her even as Joran's fear spiked.

Whatever he did got its attention alright.

The serpent slithered away, smashing through a building in its haste to reach him.

"Joran! Meet me in the city center!"

Mia sprinted to get into position. Luckily the run took only seconds. The only item of interest was a statue of the emperor in the middle of the plaza. Not an ideal hiding place, but it would have to serve.

She got out of sight just as Joran came running into view. His racing heart nearly made her faint.

The serpent followed only a few yards behind as he rushed toward the statue.

He stumbled and went to his knees.

The serpent slithered forward mouth open and fangs dripping.

This was it.

As it came down to swallow Joran whole, she darted out and braced the spear on the cobblestones.

The monster had no time to slow.

It impaled itself on the spear.

The massive head snapped back and it roared.

Mia hastened to get Joran to his feet. The two of them fled to the far side of the plaza as the serpent thrashed around, destroying nearby buildings and tearing up stones.

"I thought you said the poison would kill it instantly."

"To be fair, it's a giant black serpent that's been sleeping in a pool of molten lava for possibly hundreds or thousands of years. It might be tougher than your average creature."

As if it heard them, the serpent turned their way.

Mia got ready to run. With neither spear nor poison, continuing the fight was suicide.

A shudder ran through the serpent, it went rigid, and collapsed. Its head ended up only half a stride from where they stood.

"Maybe not instant, but that was still pretty fast."

"Don't brag, it's unbecoming."

Joran grinned. "Maybe you'll get along better with my mother than I first thought."

———

J oran and Mia barely had time to gather themselves when Alexandra came running into the plaza. She had outdistanced her guards by a good four strides. No doubt they'd be annoyed by that, not that anyone dared complain to the princess.

He opened his mouth to greet her when Alexandra wrapped her arms around him, nearly tackling him to the ground. "You did it! Killing that serpent saved thousands of lives."

"Not me, Majesty." Joran had no idea what to do with his hands. Normally having a beautiful woman hugging him would be less awkward, but when the woman was the emperor's daughter, it got more complicated. "Mia did all the hard work. I mostly offered moral support."

Alexandra promptly released him and hugged Mia. The sudden rush of pleasure that blasted through their link nearly overwhelmed Joran. Even if she had come to understand how Alexandra used people, the desire remained. Probably it always would despite the knowledge that nothing would ever come of it.

When Alexandra stepped away from Mia, his soulmate's face had flushed to the ears and her mouth hung partway open. Not a particularly good look, but the princess pretended not to notice.

"You're both heroes as far as I'm concerned. We'll have statues made for each of you, to put beside Father's." She glanced at the dead serpent. It had collapsed on the emperor's statue, smashing it to pieces. "We'll get three made. Just as soon as we figure out how to get this thing cut up and out of here."

Alexandra kicked the serpent and a tremor ran through it.

The Iron Guards scrambled to get between her and the serpent.

They needn't have worried. Instead of rising up to strike them all down, it collapsed in on itself, turned to black dust, and dissolved into the earth. In moments only the shattered pieces of Mia's spear remained in the plaza. Aside from the damage, no sign of the monster remained.

"Did you know it was going to do that?" Mia asked.

"No. What I know about the serpent wouldn't fill the first page of my journal. There's so much left to learn I'm not sure where to begin. Unraveling all the mysteries we uncovered here might take a lifetime."

"I doubt Samaritan will give us that long," Mia said.

Joran couldn't argue with that. But for now he had more immediate concerns. "Majesty, would it be possible to talk somewhere more comfortable? I'm about done in."

Alexandra laughed like a delighted child on Solstice morning. "Of course. If anyone's earned a rest, it's you two. I have a few orders to dispatch then we'll meet in my quarters. Don't forget, there's still the matter of your rewards."

Joran had no need for rewards, not with his family's wealth, but maybe Mia wanted something. He certainly knew one thing she wanted, but he sent a silent prayer to The One God that she didn't ask for it. Alexandra would be apt to send her to a post on the far side of the empire.

———

From his hiding place in the jungle, Samaritan watched the serpent die through his farseer. How had they done it? All his research said the creature should have been virtually invincible. Certainly it had shrugged off the alchemist's fire easily enough. How he wished he could have seen the faces of the arrogant imperials when their most cherished weapon failed.

No doubt some new weapon had brought about the serpent's death. If the empire excelled at one thing, it was finding new ways to kill. But no matter. He had many paths to victory. If this one had failed, he'd move on to the next. Even if it took a hundred years, he'd find a way to bring the empire to its knees.

He pulled a silver amulet out of the folds of his tunic. It had The One God's circle symbol with a slash through it. The cult of The One True God had proven useful. Their leader hated the empire nearly as much as Samaritan himself. Their first meeting had been like siblings getting reacquainted after a long time apart. He'd shared his research and she gave him access to her network of spies and saboteurs.

He'd need to speak with them eventually, but for now he'd return to his private lair to rest and plan his next move.

Samaritan closed his eyes and rubbed the amulet. Ether gathered around him, passing through the metal before entering his chest and spreading through his limbs. When the pain grew to the point he feared he might explode, he vanished.

Quick as thought he appeared in an empty stone room with a circle drawn on the floor. The intricate design had been there when he found it several years ago and it had taken him months to figure out how to use it. But now he had an unstoppable escape route.

He staggered and fell to one knee. Of course, as with all good things, this one came with a price. But a day of exhaustion and uselessness seemed a small-enough price to pay. It certainly was compared to the one the empire would pay when he finished with them.

CHAPTER 26

J oran sat on the couch in Alexandra's quarters, a glass of chilled wine in his hand and one of the servants working the kinks out of his neck and shoulders. The young lady knew her business. Joran hadn't felt this relaxed since leaving Tiber. Even Mia had her feet up on a stool, though her sword stayed within easy reach.

A full day had passed since they killed the serpent and Alexandra still hadn't returned from sending her few messages. Joran assumed that if another major threat had appeared someone would have let him know. Since no one had, he happily relaxed and enjoyed the fruits of victory.

Doubtless some demon heard his happy thoughts for not a moment later the door swung open and Alexandra strode through. She looked less pleased than he'd expected considering the province was now largely secured.

"Something wrong?" Joran asked.

"Those idiots want to resume the war with the natives. Now that one tribe has been dealt with they think the rest should go down easier. There's a hole in the city wall big enough to march a legion through and they want to start another fight. The One God save me from moron generals."

Joran sat up and nearly spilled his wine. "Did you speak to Antius? The whole fight with the lizardmen was orchestrated by a madman calling himself Samaritan. I've already talked to the lizardmen's chief. They want peace as much as we do. A few days of negotiations should get you everything you want without further bloodshed."

Alexandra dropped into the empty chair and a servant brought her chilled wine without having to be asked. "The problem is, the generals want bloodshed. It's their purpose in life. By the way, Caius made it back in one piece. That has to be some kind of miracle. I figured he'd drop dead of heat exhaustion on the hike through the jungle, assuming the serpent didn't eat him."

"Isn't the army's purpose to secure the empire?" Mia asked. "Pointless fighting only costs us warriors and potential citizens. Bringing the natives into the empire peacefully gains the emperor far more."

Alexandra grinned and turned to Joran. "You're a good influence on her. I can put them off until the city is secure. Can you get me a peace treaty by then?"

"With Draq's help, I think I can. But before I leave, there's another matter we need to discuss." Joran glanced at the servants.

Alexandra waved the women away and when the three of them were alone asked, "That bad?"

"I don't know how bad it is, but I certainly didn't want anyone else hearing what I have to say. The one called Samaritan—Antius knows something about him. He wouldn't tell me anything and basically said to keep my nose out of church business. According to Draq, Samaritan dressed like a White

Knight. Makes me wonder if we have a renegade on our hands. He certainly had some training at the imperial college."

Alexandra leaned her head back and stared at the ceiling. "Ugh. I need a fight with the church only slightly more than I need another giant serpent. Do you suppose we could just let the church deal with him?"

"Sure, but considering the lengths Samaritan went to in order to hurt the empire, I doubt he'll just stop. We may not have a choice about whether we end up facing him again."

She sat up and shot him a mock glare. "You're just a font of good news. Anything else I need to know?"

"No, I think that's it." Joran offered a sheepish smile. "I don't mean to add to your burden, truly."

"I'm sure you don't. Now go get me a peace treaty." Alexandra shooed them toward the door. "Feel free to use our usual dragon ship."

It said something about his expanded resistance to fear that the idea of going back up in the dragon ship didn't even make his knees wobble. Whether that was a good thing or not, he hadn't decided.

———

Draq must have been watching for their arrival as the gondola had barely set them at the edge of the battle-field when the lizardman came striding out of the jungle. Joran found the sight of him much more comforting than many of the humans he knew.

"Friend Joran, you survived." Draq bobbed his head in what Joran took as a sign of respect. "I held out few hopes. The angry one didn't come with you?"

Joran chuckled. "No, Antius stayed in the city. No doubt praying for something. How are your people?"

"Both of our remaining villages are safe. Most of our warriors died here, but many strong juveniles survived. We will rebuild." Draq's eyes narrowed. "Will we have to teach them to fight your empire?"

"Not if you join it. That's why I'm here. If we can work out a peace treaty, your tribe's safety will be assured as will the safety of any other tribe that signs."

"What must we do?" Draq cocked his head. "Peace with the empire has a price. This, I believe, may be the one true thing Samaritan told us."

"That's true." Joran took a deep breath. "You need to agree to abide by the empire's laws and not harm its people. You also have to agree to worship The One God. Trade deals can be worked out with individual merchant companies. Den Cade Trading will do right by you, I guarantee it."

"My people worship the spirits of the land and have forever. I can't simply order them to stop."

"I've been thinking about that. What you can do is claim that you've come to understand that the spirits are messengers of The One God and through them you worship him. It's a fine distinction but should satisfy the priests. They'll send missionaries eventually to build churches in your villages. They'll bring healing potions and tell you about all the wonders of their religion. As long as you play along and don't kill anyone, it should be fine."

Draq scratched the rapidly fading scar on his side. "That should be doable. As prices for peace go, it's small enough."

"Will the other tribes agree?" Joran asked.

"I can send messengers and ask. But I have no control over their decisions. The tribes are fiercely independent."

"Okay. I beg you to make it clear to them that some of the generals want war and anyone that isn't part of the empire will make an acceptable target for their bloodlust. Our chief is doing her best to keep them under control, but only the treaty can make you permanently safe. At least from us."

"I will share your words. What should we do if we agree?"

"Bring them here and we'll return to the city together. I'll visit every few days until you arrive. When we reach the city, I'll introduce you to Alexandra and you can sign the treaty with her. Once that's done, your people are secure. I wish you the best of luck."

Draq bobbed his head again, started to turn, then paused. "Why does your empire want the jungle? Humans are hardly meant to live here. You'd do better elsewhere."

"We certainly would." Joran shook his head and chuckled at the absurdity of the situation. "The empire has only one goal, conquer the world and in doing so bring The One God's faith to every sentient being. Until that is done, we'll never stop. It's not my preference, but I'm most certainly not in charge."

"Pity," Draq said. "If you were, your empire might be a sane place to live."

When Draq had gone Mia touched his arm. "That was a rather cynical explanation."

He shrugged and waved a glow light at the dragon ship. "Maybe, but as long as they agree to the treaty and no one else dies, I don't care."

CHAPTER 27

The leaders of the other lizardman tribes gathered at the battle site less than a month after Joran spoke to Draq. Joran spotted the six of them as soon as the dragon ship arrived in the airspace above the battlefield. They didn't get there a moment too soon. The legions had worked furiously to rebuild Cularo and it wouldn't be long before they completed repairs on the wall. Many of the civilians had returned as well which came as a surprise. After everything that happened, Joran had assumed most of them would want to return to a safer part of the empire.

Joran himself couldn't wait to return to Tiber, even knowing the work Alexandra had waiting for him. At least he could sleep in his own bed and eat familiar food. Maybe even a few hours in the lab each week would be possible.

"Are we really bringing those savages aboard the ship, my lord?" the captain asked.

"Indeed we are, Captain. And remember, if all goes well, those savages will be provincial citizens in a few hours."

The captain's face twisted in distaste. No surprise there

since from his bronze skin and dark hair Joran recognized him as a true imperial not a provincial. The frequent and casual arrogance of those born in the homeland around Tiber never ceased to amaze and depress Joran. For the empire to survive and thrive, that needed to change. Not that he had any real hope.

Joran and Mia made their way down to the hold and boarded the gondola. It took a moment to find the translation potion in his kit and when he did, he drank it down. The addition of the detect-deception element left a bitter aftertaste, but he'd drunk far worse potions over the years.

Mia kept her hand close to the hilt of her sword. Her tension came loud and clear through their link. Joran appreciated her focus. Having her at his back made this much easier than it would have been on his own.

"You think this is a trap?" she asked.

"No, but I've been wrong plenty of times." Joran showed her the vial hidden in his left hand. "You're not the only one ready for it."

"What does that do?"

"Nothing fatal. It'll paralyze them for half an hour or so. Even better, I'm already immune to this one, so hopefully you are as well."

She shot him a look. "Hopefully?"

"I told you I wanted to test this kind of thing. Relax, I've got an antidote as well."

The gondola settled on the ground and Draq came over first. "Welcome back, friend Joran."

"Thank you. I didn't think you'd spread the word so quickly."

"I took your warning to heart. Once I spoke with the nearest chieftain, we used a spirit messenger to reach the others. We all agreed that peace would be good. The shamans even agreed that calling the spirits messengers from your god wouldn't upset them or cause offense."

Joran wiped sweat from his brow. "That's far better than I hoped. Shall we board and return to the city? My chief is eager to meet you."

That last bit was a total exaggeration, but Alexandra did want to end the fighting as soon as possible.

The other chieftains eyed the gondola with much the same distrust as Joran, but finally they climbed aboard. Mia entered last and closed the door.

As they rose, one of the other chiefs asked, "How long will this take?"

"Not long. A little over an hour to fly back, and Her Majesty should be waiting nearby for our arrival. Once you both sign the treaty, you can either leave via the front gate or we can fly you back. Your choice."

"I will walk," a different chief said in a growling voice, drawing many nods of agreement.

Joran didn't blame them. Though he had finally gotten used to traveling by dragon ship, he still didn't exactly enjoy flying.

The gondola locked in place and the dragon ship started to turn for Cularo. For everyone's comfort and wellbeing, Joran decided that remaining in the hold would be best. The few crewmen on duty eyed the lizardmen with apprehension and it appeared to be mutual. Not the best start, but at least no one drew steel or bared their claws.

"Will the empire truly leave us in peace after this meeting?" Draq asked. He sounded desperate to have his decision reaffirmed.

"They will. Despite some of our more bloodthirsty leaders, most don't want to see anyone die needlessly. It's a big world, my friend." Joran smiled and clapped Draq on the shoulder. "Considering all that needs to be done, you probably won't see another human for years after this. And if you do, just be nice, like you're all part of one big tribe."

Draq offered the little bob of respect. He seemed to like the analogy.

A little less than an hour later the dragon ship started to descend. Not long after that they were tied off and Joran stood at the top of the ramp. Outside he saw no sign of Alexandra or any of the generals. The latter suited him fine, but the former made him nervous. If she'd changed her mind, he didn't know what would happen.

He let out the breath he'd been holding when Alexandra came stomping out of the keep with her Iron Guards on her heels. She looked a bit like a storm cloud about to thunder. Two of the guards carried a table while a third looked like he had writing supplies.

"This can't be good." Mia's gaze shifted toward the sky. "There's a dragon ship incoming."

Joran glanced up and sure enough a dragon ship was making its way right toward them. Since both their ships were in the yard, this one was probably coming from the capital. He did his best not to think about what might have happened and turned his focus back to Alexandra.

"Trouble, Majesty?" he asked.

"Just the usual stupidity from my generals." She stalked up the ramp and paused beside him. "I had to remind them that they fought who we told them to fight. Caius in particular seemed to think that killing some natives would bring the Fifth back to its former glory. I informed him that if he kept giving me a hard time, a different general would be overseeing the rebuilding. Now, let's get this treaty signed. I've wasted enough time on this province."

The guards hastened to set the table up and unroll the treaty. Joran read it to the chiefs. It said exactly what he'd told them it would, thank The One God. Though they didn't know how to write in Imperial script, each of the tribes had its own symbol. That suited Alexandra and when they finished, she signed her name as well.

"Welcome to the empire," she said.

Joran translated and the lizardmen each made the little bobbing bow they favored.

"Do we need to do anything else, friend Joran?" Draq asked.

"No, as Her Majesty said, you're all part of the empire now. Just to be on the safe side, Mia and I will walk you to the gate so there are no misunderstandings. We were at war not that long ago after all. It will take time for the bad feelings to subside." And for some Joran seriously doubted they ever would.

The incoming dragon ship was only a quarter mile or so away now. Though curious, Joran wanted to get the lizardmen out of the city before anything happened. They went to the southern gate since he didn't want to risk running into the blacksmith whose family they killed. Somehow Joran doubted the man would appreciate the peace treaty at the moment.

The One God must have been watching over them as they reached the gate with no issues and with a final wave goodbye, the chiefs took their leave.

"That's a relief," Mia said, speaking his thoughts out loud.

"It certainly is. Hopefully the peace will hold and we can get the hell out of Stello Province."

She grinned. "The jungle hasn't grown on you?"

"Not hardly."

The walk back to the government building was considerably less tense than the walk out and they arrived just as the dragon ship touched down. Alexandra stood nearby which surprised Joran. They moved over to join her.

"I figured you'd be back inside having a drink," he said.

"Doubtless whoever's on board will wish to speak with me. Might as well make it easy for them."

"Thoughtful of you."

"Besides, given the mood I'm in now, I'm apt to run through the first general that crosses my path."

That sounded more like her.

The ramp dropped before the ground crew had finished tying down the ship and a single man in crimson and gold livery hurried down. He focused on Alexandra who had stiffened at the sight of him.

"Who is it?" Joran asked.

"An official imperial messenger. Only Father or Marcus have the authority to send one. Something must have happened in the capital."

The messenger took a knee in front of Alexandra. "I bear a message from His Imperial Highness Marcus Tiberius the Twenty-Seventh for Your Majesty's ears only."

"Excuse us, Majesty." Joran offered a bow and hurried to back away.

"No!" Alexandra grabbed his sleeve in a death grip. "Joran, you stay. Everyone else, go away."

When the others, including Mia—though she could probably hear everything with her enhanced senses—had moved out of earshot Alexandra said, "Joran is my personal advisor and anything you can say to me you can say in front of him. Speak."

Joran hardly considered himself worthy of such confidence

given their short association, but maybe saving her life twice had convinced Alexandra that he had her best interests at heart.

"As you command, Majesty. His Imperial Majesty, Emperor Marcus Tiberius the Twenty-Sixth is dying. Your brother requests that you return to the capital at best speed if you wish to see him again before the end."

Alexandra fell against him and Joran did his best not to let her hit the ground. A difficult task given how wobbly his own knees felt. If the emperor was dying, that would shake the empire to its core. Given how tricky successions could be, anything might happen.

"We're leaving." Alexandra straightened, her moment of weakness gone. "Right now."

She took a step toward the new dragon ship.

Joran hesitated then said, "Maybe we should take our usual ship. It's been checked for explosives."

She turned to look at him as if suddenly remembering the threat hiding in the empire. "Good point. That's exactly why I made you my advisor. And I'm going to need you now more than ever."

Mia and the Iron Guards hurried to join them as they strode toward the dragon ship Joran had used to transport the lizardmen. The messenger trailed along behind seeming not fully certain why they were switching ships but clearly unwilling to question Alexandra.

He had been well trained.

As soon as they were on board the order to return to the capital went up to the bridge. Joran had no idea what they were flying into, but he feared it might be more dangerous than the war with the lizardmen.

AUTHOR NOTE

Hello everyone,

And so we've come to the end of The Unwelcome Journey. The trouble is only beginning for our heroes as Book 2 will bring them to the heart of the empire where a new threat is lurking in the shadows.

I hope you'll join me next time when Joran, Mia, and Alexandra's adventure continues in Darkness in Tiber.

You can find links to all my books on my website, www.jamesewisher.com

Thanks for reading and I'll see you next time.

James

ALSO BY JAMES E WISHER

The Soul Bound Saga
An Unwelcome Journey
Darkness in Tiber
Depths of Betrayal
The Black Iron Empire
Overmage

The Divine Key Trilogy
Shadow Magic
For The Greater Good
The Divine Key Awakens

The Portal Wars Saga
The Hidden Tower
The Great Northern War
The Portal Thieves
The Master of Magic
The Chamber of Eternity
The Heart of Alchemy
The Sanguine Scroll

The Dragonspire Chronicles
The Black Egg
The Mysterious Coin

The Four Nations Tournament

Death Incarnate

Atlantis Rising

Rise of the Demon Lords

The Pale Princess

Aegis of Merlin Omnibus Vol 1.

Aegis of Merlin Omnibus Vol 2.

The Complete Aegis of Merlin Omnibus

Other Fantasy Novels:

The Squire

Death and Honor Omnibus

The Rogue Star Series:

Children of Darkness

Children of the Void

Children of Junk

Rogue Star Omnibus Vol. 1

Children of the Black Ship

ABOUT THE AUTHOR

James E. Wisher is a writer of science fiction and fantasy novels. He's been writing since high school and reading everything he could get his hands on for as long as he can remember.

To learn more:
www.jamesewisher.com
james@jamesewisher.com

CPSIA information can be obtained
at www.ICGtesting.com
Printed in the USA
BVHW040639220223
658982BV00001B/4